V

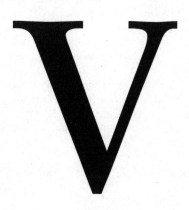

Agent Provocateur

V

THE SECRET LIFE OF V

AN EROTIC NOVELLA

PAVILION

First published in Great Britain in 2007 by
PAVILION BOOKS
151 Freston Road, London W10 6TH

An imprint of Anova Books Company Ltd

Text © Anova Books Company Ltd, 2007

Author: Neo
Typesetting and jacket design: Lotte Oldfield
Copyeditor: Ian Allen
Proofreader: Kate Burkhalter

A CIP catalogue record for this book is available from the
British Library.

ISBN 9781862057470

Printed and bound by MPG Books Ltd, Bodmin, Cornwall

10 9 8 7 6 5 4 3 2

This book can be ordered direct from the publisher.
Contact the marketing department, but try your bookshop first.

CONTENTS

PREFACE

In 2006 we published our first series of erotic fiction, *Secrets* and *Confessions*, judging there to be a huge gap in the market for sexy provocative literature, primarily aimed at women, which was neither smutty nor prurient, but instead revelled in erotic possibility and crafted its prose with care and elegance. The packaging was important too, as we wanted to create hardback books to be proud of and to display by the bedside, not grubby paperbacks to hide under the bed.

We were rewarded in 2006 when this collection of erotic shorts was announced the winner of the prestigious Erotic Award for literature.

Now we have decided to push the boundaries a little further with these novellas, which will allow the reader to begin a long journey with two enigmatic and liberated characters. The result is another pair of astoundingly frank erotic adventures which we hope stimulate the Agent Provocateur in you.

Joseph Corré and Serena Rees, 2007

INTRODUCTION

Men want to sleep with their female best friends.
Women love talking to a male best friend in a way they
never can with their partners. Sometimes everyone
gets what they want . . .

I

V IS FOR VARIETY

V tells me everything. Some of her stories stay with me as though I were there. Some I can never forget . . .

'I buy you drink.'

Is it a question or a demand? V doesn't know. She thinks for a second. She doesn't want to know. She's intrigued enough by the words. 'Let's see where this goes,' she thinks. Out loud, she says, 'OK.'

She looks at the cocktail menu in front of her. Suddenly it's taken away by the barman. In its place a small round paper mat is dropped down and a sugar-rimmed Martini glass stood on top of it. V is confused. She hasn't chosen yet. She's not sure she's in a Martini mood.

As the smart, red-shirted barman works the cocktail shaker vigorously above his right shoulder and then his left, V glimpses at the stranger next to her. He is leaning on the counter, looking straight at the barman, not at her. A cigarette burns languorously from his left hand. Like a lot of the Japanese businessmen she has met, this one seems to have the weight of the world embedded in the deep furrows of his brow. His face contains more stories than the Tokyo library. He looks doleful. Smart – smart enough to be allowed into this bar – and rich enough, certainly, but definitely doleful. What's eating him up, V wonders. What's his history?

The barman is the height of efficiency and strains the perfect vodka Martini into her glass without splashing a drop. A cherry and wooden stirrer complete the effect.

The businessman grunts, and the bartender pours another perfect drink into his prepared glass. Another grunt and the barman scurries away. It's not the first time V has been in Tokyo, not by any means, but she'll never tire of being fascinated by the quiet and respectful efficiency shown by the waiting staff to their regulars.

'Kampai,' the customer says. He turns as he says it and raises his glass high above his head in her direction. Seated, she towers above him. Some men, especially some Japanese men, are intimidated by her height. But not this man. If he notices the difference, he doesn't show it.

'What are we drinking?' V asks.

The man stares at his glass as though it holds the mysteries of the universe. 'This is drink for men and women,' he says in his punchy, efficient English. 'This is drink for friends.' V raises an eyebrow at this. 'This is drink for lovers.'

So there we have it, she thinks. That is what he's up to. It's not the first time a run-down businessman has tried his luck with her. Hopefully it won't be the last. But she didn't see this coming. It's two in the morning. He was alone at the hotel bar when she came in for some ice to take to her room. She had no intention of stopping. No intention of sitting down until he had spoken to her. Or rather, until he had spoken at her.

There was a directness to his words and his actions that appealed to her. Especially after the evening she'd had. Banquets with high-flying investors and international bankers provided good food, but little by way of conversation or, at least on this occasion, other distractions. And everyone she had met tonight had loved the sound of his own voice too much for her to enjoy. This guy was different. This guy had his own agenda and it had nothing to do with share prices. He didn't even seem too bothered about being liked. And far from loving it, the sound of his voice seemed like an expensive seasoning to him, to be used sparingly.

'Why you up?' he barks at her.

'I was at a business meeting.'

'You, business?' The derision in the man's voice

cannot be masked. He doesn't try to. 'What business? Lady business?'

The penny drops. He thinks she works the hotels. And why shouldn't he? She's on her own, in a strange country, appearing next to a single man at a bar in the middle of the night. In his country, only one type of woman keeps those sorts of hours. Only one type of woman can afford the dress she's wearing.

V decides to put his mind at rest. 'My husband is a director of a business,' she says. 'He takes me along to functions to look nice.'

She knows as soon as she utters the words that she has just confirmed her new friend's stereotype of her. And honestly, can she blame him? He doesn't know that her husband is gay, that he needs her as his trophy wife to keep the narrow-minded business contacts from walking away. He doesn't know that her husband has a Valium dependency to keep his coke habit in check. He doesn't know that their's is a relationship drawn up in a solicitor's office by two old friends trying to help each other. He doesn't know any of this, but if he did he would shrug and say, 'I was right.'

The realization of the way V's life is turning out rocks her. Then she remembers it was her idea. That she was the one who needed an escape route from the life she had been living and Lord LH had been there for her. That this arrangement gives her total freedom to be who she wants to be, with whom she wants. That she has no money worries, that she is the darling of the monthly press, that she has the opportunity for all the excitement a woman like her craves.

But there's always room for some more.

It will only take one of those guys from the dinner to find their way up to this penthouse bar, she thinks, and I'll be fried. But they'll all be with their hookers tonight. She knows this to be likely, based on past experience. But the possibility that it might not happen that way tonight excites her. She's only talking to this stranger, but in Japan, in business circles at least, that's as good as dropping to your knees in front of him. Lord LH would not be happy. And neither would his shareholders.

'You don't like your drink?' It's another question that could be an instruction.

V realizes she has barely touched a drop. She waves her hand to say no, it's fine, and takes a sip. And another. The shallow glass is drained within seconds.

'I will get the next one,' she says, and looks for the barman.

Her companion makes another grunt sound, a man appears from a curtain to the side and service is resumed.

'We'll have two Martinis please,' she says.

It's almost imperceptible, but V catches the

bartender's eye as he glances instinctively over to the Japanese next to her. An affirmative gesture is made and the barman smiles and gives V a shallow nod.

V is surprised when the barman serves up three glasses this time, not two. She is even more surprised when a glamorous Japanese woman appears beside her and picks one up.

'Kampai,' she says, and clinks glasses with V.

The businessman takes control. 'This is Keiko,' he says. 'She is artist. Very famous. She has show in Europe, in Germany. Very good.'

Keiko steps back and drapes her arm around the man. She doesn't take her eyes off V for a second, not even when she kisses the ear of her friend.

'I paint glass,' she says. 'Beautiful glass, ornaments and windows. But nothing as beautiful as you.'

'Your English is very good,' V says, and regrets the words instantly. She hates people who judge intelligence on how well they speak a certain tongue.

'Thank you,' Keiko says. 'I was born in Paris, raised in Berlin. But here is home. Here is where I make my art, and meet my lovers.'

Again that word. V can see from the way the couple locks arms, hers around his neck, his around her waist, that they are lovers. He must have been waiting for her to return. Any conversation with V was small talk. How foolish. She had misread the signs.

Occasionally it happens, but this time she had felt so sure. It must have been the champagne downstairs that had clouded her judgement. The guy was just being friendly.

'Keiko art very beautiful.' The man looks at his partner. 'Like Keiko. Very beautiful.' He lets his hand drop from her waist and on to her small bottom. 'You want to see?' he asks.

V isn't sure if he's still talking about his girlfriend's art. But she says yes. She expects to be shown a portfolio of images from the man's attaché case. She expects him to perhaps produce some pictures from his wallet.

But she doesn't expect him to reach up to the strap of Keiko's shoulderless dress and tear it down violently. Keiko doesn't flinch, but V nearly falls off her stool. She is aware of her Martini soaking her lap, but she doesn't look down at the stain on her dress or her empty glass. She doesn't take her eyes away from the vision standing before her.

Keiko is no more than five feet tall. Her long black hair is pinned to one side of her head, and she wears the smallest, daintiest underwear. To V's Western eye, the tiny yet ornate bra and panties look like doll's clothes. But she can tell from Keiko's eyes that this is no doll.

This is all woman.

The man tugs at the dress again and it falls completely to the floor. Keiko takes one step to the side, then kicks the discarded frock away. Her heels mask her true height by three or four inches. Her stockingless legs are blemish-free and golden. Her waist tucks perfectly in above her 28-inch hips, then pushes out again and into her tiny ribs and, above, her small but underwired breasts.

V is suddenly aware of the bartender still near her. So is the man. He grunts again and the barkeep disappears behind his curtain. A second later he reappears from behind V and bends down to retrieve the torn dress. Before he can stand, Keiko places a foot on his back. The bartender pauses, unsure of what to do. V watches as he looks at the standing leg by his head, and raises his eyes up, to the nearby knee, and higher. Keiko is so tiny the crouched man can take in all her charms without straining. Whatever he is thinking, V guesses, he is enjoying the view.

Something is said in Japanese and V senses a sigh of resignation from the man on his knees. Keiko is looking at her. 'Come,' she says. 'Let me see how tall you are.'

V slides out of the bucket stool and steps towards the two strangers and their genuflecting servant. She towers above both of them, wondering what they have in mind. And then she finds out.

Placing one hand firmly on the businessman's shoulder, Keiko presses her foot further into the bartender's back, then pushes herself up fully on to him. V hears the man gasp, then shout. The long shoe heels are like acupuncture needles in his back. This man is in pain. But he dare not move. This much is obvious. Someone has a hold over him.

Keiko struggles to gain her balance. She looks like a novitiate surfer, but as she leans further on her friend, her face quickly regains its composure. Something else is said in Japanese, and this time it is accompanied by a definite stamp from the needle-thin heels. The man on his knees lets out a cry. Then nothing. He is broken.

V notices that she and Keiko are now the same height. Their eyes lock. It is a game, a challenge. Who will give in first? What will happen to the loser? What will be the winner's prize?

'You want more drink?' This time it is a question from the businessman. V is still holding her empty glass. 'Yes, please,' she says. 'I'd like that.' Then she pauses. 'But who is going to make it?'

'Have mine,' he says, and he throws the contents of his glass towards Keiko. The Martini hits her torso and splashes her face, her neck and even V. V watches as the alcohol runs down the diminutive body in front of her and drips onto the man beneath her feet. For the first time this evening her excitement sends a tingle throughout her body. She feels it around her shoulders and down her arms. The hairs on the back of her neck start to prickle. She is beginning to enjoy this.

'You drink now,' the man barks, and V knows what to do. She leans forwards, bends her legs and lets her tongue land in Keiko's bellybutton. A small pool of Martini is her reward, and she quickly sucks it into her mouth. The sound she makes is that of a kiss.

'Good,' the man says. 'Drink more.'

V begins to straighten, and lets her tongue follow a sour vodka rivulet up Keiko's stomach, taking in as much as she can swallow without breaking her motion. She reaches the small, diamond-encrusted bra and runs her tongue first left, then right, under each cup. She is surprised at how much the expensive fabric has soaked up. She bites against it and sucks vigorously. She moves an inch and repeats the action. Each time a new drop, another mouthful.

She feels Keiko's arms move before she sees them. A moment later the bra is released and falls on her face. Its remaining liquid drips onto her face and she wipes it off with the back of a hand.

Keiko's breasts are prominently pert, with brown cherry nipples tilting at the sky. Although small, they quiver tantalizingly as she tries to maintain her balance. They are much smaller than V's own breasts, and much darker. But right now, they are the only breasts in the world and V must have them.

Putting a leg over the barman, she stands astride him. Still without moving her gaze, she lowers herself until she feels the tense muscle of the underling's back beneath her. She feels the minute tremors rocking his body as he fights to carry Keiko's weight, as he concentrates on banishing all thought of pain from his mind. A minute ago V wished she could help him. Now she barely knows he's there as she takes her seat on his back. She couldn't care less about him or anything else. She only cares about the tiny Japanese in front of her.

She edges forwards and feels the barman's shirt crumple as her weight drags it out of his trousers. She is inches from Keiko. Her breasts hang just above the girl's knees; another movement and they would rest against them. V reaches out and lets her hands glide against Keiko's hips, the silk of the panties soft to the palm's touch. But V doesn't stop. Her hands keep moving, until she can no longer see them behind the girl, and suddenly she feels her fingers meet. She smiles. Slowly V moves her touching hands down and imagines the view the businessman has, of her tanned fingers folding down like blinds lowering over the bristling, firm cheeks of the girl. The cut of Keiko's panties is classic brief, and it is a few seconds before

V's blind touch brushes against skin again. But when it happens, she lingers. She halts all movement, conscious of the rush of blood spiralling around her own body. In that slight movement, in that act of skin meeting skin, a cyclone is set off inside her. She feels its fury around her lungs as her breathing becomes more difficult. She feels it around her stomach as nerves make themselves known for the first time. And she feels it between her legs, where the tornado's source focuses its power.

A tremor from Keiko disturbs V's reverie. Perhaps the barman shifted his weight, perhaps she lost her footing. Or perhaps she was growing impatient with her caresser's delay?

V looks up for the first time at the pretty, perfectly symmetrical face staring down. Keiko's tongue darts out and stays locked between her teeth. She looks impish, game for anything. But impatient to begin.

V pokes her own tongue out, but then she looks away. With her tongue still exposed, she leans forwards and tastes for the first time the perfumes on the young Japanese skin, the cinnamon bath oils massaged into her tender form, and still a trace of vodka. She kisses the girl lightly at the top of her stomach, then moves lower, kissing again, lower still, more ghosted butterfly touches with her lips.

At the same time she slides her hands back around the tiny hips, leading with her thumbs, letting her fingers trail behind, soaking up the flesh, embracing in the tennis ball shape. Keiko is small, but not boyish. Her bottom is not large, but not flat. Her curves are real, but distinctly feminine.

As V's hands draw closer to the front, she lets her thumbs meet at the centre of the waistband. She lowers her head and kisses the area just above. She does it again, kissing below this time. Like the bra earlier, the silk is soft with the damp of Martini. Each kiss goes lower, and each time she sucks lightly to soak up the drink. As her head drops, so do her thumbs, moving down over the front of the panties, making small circular motions as they move. Her touch is light, barely making an impression on the silk. But they make an impression on the skin beneath. V does not need to speak Japanese to understand the soft utterances coming from the entranced face above her. Short gasps, quiet intakes of breath followed by elongated exhalations.

With her next kiss, V takes the silk between her teeth and bites down. Keiko squeals and automatically drops one hand down on to V's head and takes a handful of hair. V hurt her. She caught more than silk between her teeth. She caught flesh. Very delicate flesh.

With the tug on her hair V halts. But only for a second. She continues the movements with her thumbs and prepares for another kiss. This time she licks the fabric afterwards and feels the grip on her head release. She repeats the action and Keiko releases her hold.

And then she bites.

'No!' Again, the small Japanese hand grasps V's head, this time sinking exquisitely manicured nails into her scalp.

This time V does not stop. She bites again. And again.

Each time the pull on her hair increases and the pain of the nails digging into her head burns. But she is in charge here.

'No!' Keiko screams. 'No!'

But still V does not stop, and all the while her thumbs get lower and lower. Lower and lower. Keiko's voice tells its own story.

'No, no, no. Oh, oooh.'

V smiles. She is playing a dangerous game. This couple, this pair of strangers, is quite willing to humiliate and hurt a local worker. They would think nothing of turning their imaginations on her if she annoyed them. But this is worth it, she thinks. This is worth the risk. This is worth any risk.

Her thumbs press harder now, sinking deeper into Keiko's warm flesh. The barman stirs as she shifts her balance, trying to move her feet further apart. She wants V to go further, to explore more of her, to discover everything.

V moves in closer, and kisses once again. Pulling her new plaything's buttocks towards her, she lets her face press against the girl's flesh beneath the underwear. She continues to kiss, but her touch is so light as to be ignored. A new sensation is flooding Keiko, a new tormentor is working on her.

The bridge of V's nose nestles against Keiko's pubic bone and for a moment she considers how much it would hurt if the barman fell, and the two female bodies were pitched violently against each other. It would hurt V more than Keiko. But this is worth it, she thinks. This is worth the risk. This is worth any risk.

She releases the pressure on Keiko's bottom and gives her own nose the freedom to run its forceful but soft tip against every delectable part hiding beneath the silk. V is a meticulous explorer, covering every inch. From the change in pitch of Keiko's squeals, she is far from lost. She knows exactly where she is. There are no secrets here.

While still pushing her face into Keiko's groin, V reaches up and allows her hand to fall on Keiko's shoulder. She rests there for a second, then lets her fingertips drag along like ghosts, up the neck until she finds an ear, then a face. She feels Keiko turn into her hand, pushing and rubbing, like a cat controlling the pressure as it rubs along your leg; on the face of it the passive partner, but all along calling the shots.

V plays awhile with Keiko's face, and lets her fingers trace the lines of her jaw, the small nub button of her nose, the surprisingly long eyelashes, the thin skin of her ear lobes and finally the full voluptuousness of her lips. As soon as the fingers get within reach, Keiko engulfs two of them, and sucks. Her tongue swirls expertly around the nails, working down past the first knuckle, then the second, to finally the hand itself. All the while Keiko groans, aware of the buried nose pleasuring her elsewhere.

V gradually draws her fingers out of Keiko's mouth. As they hit the air-conditioned room she feels a sudden coolness. Perfect, she thinks, for what she has in mind. She runs the palm of her hand down over Keiko's chin, down her neck and over her collarbone. She is close to Keiko's breasts, she must be, if she moves left or right. She chooses right and instantly feels the springy firmness of youthful resistance under her touch. With one movement, V lets her palm fall down and feels her fingers, her wet, chilled fingers, glance against the tall nipple that stands like a lighthouse against the rocks. She runs her fingertips around it, circling it one way and then the next. And then she squeezes.

Her pinch is hard. Hard enough for Keiko to cry aloud once more. Hard enough to make her plunge both hands onto V's head, solely using the lower woman's body for balance. It is reckless and painful, but V loves it. She loves the feeling that things could go very wrong. She loves the sensation of her hair close to being yanked clean from her head. And she loves the fact that she caused it all by pinching this beautiful Japanese's nipple – and might just do it again.

With a push of her head, V regains control as Keiko releases her hair. Her nose, her nuzzling, her soft kisses against the hot silk, temper Keiko's mood. She is calmed as quickly as she exploded. Without looking, V moves her hand back to the standing girl's face, looking for her mouth. To her surprise she finds another's fingers there. Keiko is licking her own fingers, sucking them.

V knows what is coming next. She can encourage it or she can prevent it.

Or she can join in.

As soon as Keiko's fingers leave her mouth, V forces her own in. By the time Keiko's hand snakes down her tummy, hooks under the waistband of her panties and slides beneath, V is reaching down beneath her own dress with her free hand. As Keiko emits a soft, soothing 'oof' of realized pleasure, V too releases her own pressure valve of frustration. Her fingers slip beneath the centre of her panties and find their way expertly inside her pussy, pulling out almost instantly to bathe her clitoris in her own juices.

She can see from the shape of Keiko's hand inside her own panties that she is doing the same. If V watches and listens, she can match Keiko, movement for movement. It becomes a game of followers and leaders. And, for once, V will follow.

Keiko's silk-masked hand steadies itself at the top of her vagina, clearly pressing against her clitoris with the flat palm. Beneath her, and out of sight to the other woman, V's own hand does the same. She wants more than anything to dip her fingers inside herself, to luxuriate in her own hot vault, but she can't. Not yet. Not until Keiko says so. Not until Keiko shows her how.

Does Keiko know what power she has? Has she worked out the rules without being told she was in a game?

At last – it seems like an eternity has passed – V sees Keiko's hand move, and one finger, then another, disappears from view, forcing the back of her hand outwards as she reaches lower and lower. V can reach inside herself more easily, her position is closer, but to do so she must press against the bartender's back and that wouldn't be fair. It wouldn't be kind to make him feel her hard knuckles grate up and down his lower spine as she writhes and rides him, rolling her cheeks for greater depth, forcing her body against itself, forcing her own pussy to wrap around her fingers, to take her further inside, closer to her very centre.

It wouldn't be fair, but she does it. She can't help herself.

She watches as Keiko pulls her hand back slowly, and lets a thumb rest awkwardly pointing upwards. With her next breath, she plunges her fingers back inside, but this time her thumb is pulled over her clit. It's the perfect action and her hand is the perfect shape.

This is trickier for V, but she manages it. Her hand is shaped like a cowboy's gun as it pushes inside her. She feels her fingers, no longer flat against her perineum, but raised, one on top of each other, and she enjoys the new way she is being pulled. She enjoys the new shapes her pussy is stretched into. She enjoys the feeling of total darkness as her hand reaches up inside her, and utter light as her thumb plies down alongside her clit.

No more, she thinks. No more of this. I need to come. I need to give in, I need to fuck myself before I go crazy.

She knows Keiko is thinking the same thing. She can smell the change, she can hear the difference in her breathing. She can feel the urgency of the small Japanese hand as it bustles beneath the drenched silk in front of her face, and she can see the relentless rhythm building up, getting more powerful, more desperate, more accurate.

And then for a second she sees nothing. Her world is pitched into blackness, all light is removed. And then her vision returns. She sees light, pure white light, and feels a thousand years of laughter surge up through her body, a millennium of happiness looking for a way out of her earthly form. It's unbearable, this release of passion, of vitality, of pure energy.

It is called the climax for a good reason, she thinks. There is nothing to follow. Nothing can match that experience for raw sensation.

V focuses directly in front of her. Keiko's hand is still. Has she experienced what V has? Has she reached the same extremes within her own body and tasted the same intensity of relief? Who was the follower and who was leading?

V leans forwards and lets both hands rest on the waist of the man beneath her. His shirt is sodden. Through the sweat of exertion or the expression of fear? Or something else? Arousal, perhaps? The perspiration of lust?

V considers for a second exploring these thoughts. But she is distracted as Keiko's legs buckle and she falls clumsily off her human footstool. Before V can react, the man reaches out and scoops his young friend into a strong hug, then lowers her to the ground gracefully. She looks up at him and smiles.

He grunts and looks down. Beneath his trousers there is the pronounced shape of a large erection. Keiko looks at it and reaches down. For the first time this evening, the man loses that detached coolness that had so intrigued V in the first place. He groans as she squeezes the shaft of his cock through the constraining wool. And then he stops.

Keiko has stopped.

She looks into his eye and pats his groin twice. 'Some other time,' she says, and walks a few steps away, towards V. V attempts to raise herself from the barman, but Keiko places a hand on her shoulder and bends down to whisper in her ear.

'I hope you like my hotel, my dear,' she says. 'I'm sorry we were on different tables earlier. I thank your husband and his friends for investing.'

Investing? Of course, that's why she looks so familiar. She was at the meeting. She was one of the people LH had come to meet. V has assumed she was eye candy, like she herself was. How wrong people could be. This has been too close for comfort. A chill of doom shoots down her spine. Keiko sees it and reacts.

'Business is business,' she whispers and kisses V on the forehead. 'And pleasure is something else.'

The last time V sees Keiko she is shouting a flurry of Japanese invective at the men. Both seem to be trying to pick her clothes up first. Both seem to be failing.

V laughs and walks towards the exit. The ice can wait. She can get it tomorrow.

Or perhaps room service could deliver some?

Hmm . . .

II

V IS FOR VENUS

I love mornings. Real mornings, the early ones. The earlier the better. Not the couple of hours before lunch that most people think of. The world's too busy by then. Too crowded, too noisy.

Too many people to share it with.

I like the world to myself. I know I'm not the only one seeing the first rays of the sun skim along the Thames from the City towards Chelsea Bridge. But it feels like it.

It feels like the boats inch along for my benefit. It feels like the seagulls in from the estuary carry a message for my ears only. The skies belong to them at the moment. The aeroplanes nest for another hour or two yet.

I love London in repose. It's when she is at her most beautiful. When she is not having to please others. When she can be herself, without being driven by the demands of strangers to perform. She is everything to all people during the day and most of the night. But for a few hours she sleeps. And that is when I love her most.

That is when she is mine.

Sometimes things work out for the best. I moved to the south side of the river because I couldn't afford the north. I moved to the eleventh floor because a house reminded me of a past I was running from. I don't have curtains because I'm claustrophobic. Blinds fence you in and up here no one can see you.

It's funny how you make decisions based on negatives. Life isn't about doing things you want to do. It's about not doing things you hate.

I can see the first joggers hacking their way along the Embankment. My time is almost up. It's nearly time to hand my city over to others. It's nearly time to share her again.

It's nearly time to eat.

I walk into the kitchen area of my open-plan room to prepare the fullest of English breakfasts. I hear a shrill bleep from behind and see my house phone flashing. I turned the ringtone to mute as soon as I bought it, but it still emits one single annoying note every time someone calls. I think it thinks it's being subtle. How quaint.

I was right about it getting late. Someone else is obviously awake. I suppose I'd better answer it.

'Hello,' I say. Sometimes it's more of a question, but today it's just a statement.

'What are you wearing?'

For a second I'm taken aback. But just for a second. I know the voice. I've known it all my life.

And I know what she's like.

'Good morning, V,' I say. 'What are you doing up so early?'

'Who said I was up? But I am awake. And I'm horny.'

That's my girl. Very direct is V. And very funny.

'V, darling, when are you not horny?' I ask. 'The ravens will flee the Tower before you stop feeling frisky.'

'That is just not true.' She sounds faux offended. I imagine her in bed, propping herself up on to one elbow. 'I once went a whole weekend without getting in the slightest bit aroused.'

'You were in Wales – it doesn't count. I bet you can't think of one single other time. Admit it, there are no occasions when you stop being on simmer.'

There's a moment of silence. 'You still haven't told me what you're wearing,' she says, changing the subject.

'Well,' I reply, 'I've got a dressing gown on and that's about it.'

'That nice one or the funny Chinese print?'

'I like the Chinese print.'

'Well?'

'OK, it's the other one . . .'

'I knew it!'

'. . . but only because it's warmer.'

I hear V laugh. I don't mind her mocking me. It never seems malicious. She has a knack for putting people at ease. She has a knack for putting people in whatever mood she chooses.

Cradling the phone under my chin, I start peering into the fridge. Where are the eggs? V can talk for England. She can entertain for Europe. But I'm hungry.

'What's that noise?' she asks. 'What are you up to?'

'I was just about to make some breakfast,' I explain.

'Oh, how lovely. I thought you'd be standing at your window admiring the river.'

She knows me too well. 'The Thames and I have said our good mornings,' I say. 'It's time for others to enjoy her now.'

'You hate sharing your view with all the little people, don't you?'

I know she's trying to goad me, but I also know she's right. 'Everyone looks little from up here,' I joke. 'But yes, I can't say I enjoy watching everyone demand a piece of her. I feel like she's family now. Too many people take her for granted. They take the whole city for granted.'

'You're a funny boy, do you know that?' V says, more of a statement than a question. 'Now, back to your gown. One knot or two?'

'One bow.'

'So it could fall open?'

'It could. But I'm pretty good at bows.'

'Sleeves – rolled up or hanging down?'

'Hanging down.'

'They could get very dirty if you're cooking.'

'Yes, I suppose they could.'

'That would be a shame.'

I hear the tone in V's voice change again. She's not sitting up any longer. She's laying back, her head sunk in Egyptian cotton pillows, one arm resting on the pillow next to her ear, barely holding the phone to her mouth. But even above the clattering I'm beginning to make in the kitchen I can hear every word. I can hear every breath.

'Thinking about you in your gown makes me horny,' V says.

'I think we've covered that,' I chide, but she ignores me.

'Thinking about you cooking makes me horny too. It makes me want to touch myself.'

'Touch yourself where?' I ask.

'Everywhere. I want to feel the back of my hand drag softly across my face. I want to sense each nail as it picks across my skin, down my neck to the top of my chest.'

'Don't use your hands,' I instruct.

'But I want to.'

'Not yet. Are you under the cover?'

'I'm under a sheet.'

'Good. Put the phone on the pillow so you can hear me and grasp the top of the sheet either side of your shoulders, so it's under your chin.'

'OK.'

'Now slowly, very slowly, pull it down. Can you do that for me?'

'I think so.'

'Pull it down so carefully that you can feel the cotton drag across your horny body. So you can feel your skin being brushed by the soft fabric. Can you do that?'

'OK.'

'How does it feel?'

'It feels so soft. It feels so smooth against my neck, and down, across both shoulders at once, brushing the insides of both arms. It's like I'm being touched in so many places at once, like dozens of mouths are breathing on different parts of my skin at the same time. Oh, I can see goose bumps. It's making me cold.'

'You're cold because you're alive. Your endorphins are being stimulated by your touch. You're responding because your skin wants to be touched. It loves being touched. It needs to be touched.'

'Oh, I think you're right.'

'Keep going. Tell me how it feels now.'

'It feels so gentle. Not like a feather teased along my skin, not like somebody's hands stroking me. I'm touched in one place then another, and all at the same time. It's so soft, I can't pinpoint where I'm feeling it. It's so soft, it keeps moving and I don't know where.'

'That's good.'

'I'm pulling away from my neck now, nearly stretching my arms straight. I can just make out the top of my breasts. I'm going more slowly now, slower and slower. I'm barely moving my hands but it feels like the sheet is lapping across my skin like a giant wave. Slower and slower. I've even got goose bumps on my breasts. I can see the tiny golden hairs springing up as the sheet pulls past. Oh, the sheet's hooked on my nipples. They're so erect, the sheet can't get past. Mmm, that's nice. That's really very nice. If I pull the sheet from side to side, I can feel them getting harder. I can feel them responding to my remote touch. Ooh. They're getting bigger. I can feel my skin tightening around them. It's like they've come alive. I really want to touch them with my fingers. I want to pinch them.'

'Don't. Not yet.'

'I need to do something. This is too much. Oh, the pleasure's spreading. I can almost see it, rippling beneath the sheet. I can see it between my legs. I can feel it. I feel alive there.'

'Can you pull the sheet down over your breasts?' I whisper.

'I don't know. It's too nice where it is, just being pulled left and right, rubbing my nipples, massaging them in cotton.'

'Tell me what you're thinking about.'

'If I close my eyes I can imagine two people kneeling next to me. I can imagine them licking my nipples, at the same time, not sucking, not kissing, just licking, just moving them with their tongues, feeling their strong hot tongues gently pushing against my erect skin. I can feel them swirl their tongues around slowly, covering each part of my nipple with their warm wetness, the tip of each breast alive to the imperceptible bumps on the tongues as they brush past.'

'What else do you feel?'

'I feel my legs. They're tingling. As I pull the sheet down, they feel it more. They feel the cotton bunch up across the gap between my thighs. I feel expectation in my legs, and electricity between them. I can't really concentrate any more, not on my breasts. I want to rush now, I want to pull back the sheet, to reveal my stomach, my hips, my pussy.'

'All in good time. You have to take these things slowly. You understand, don't you?'

A grunt signifies she does. It also signifies something else. Something I haven't told her to do.

'Where are your hands?' I ask. 'Tell me, where are they?'

There is silence. Then the sound of a long, hard breath exhaled.

'Oops, silly me,' she says breathily. 'I dropped the sheet. I'm such a butterfingers. Are you cross?'

'I'm very cross,' I tell her. 'I'm going to finish my breakfast now. I'll speak to you later.'

'No!' She screams it into the phone. I smile. I was bluffing. I knew that and at any other time she would have known that. But not now. At this moment she's not sure. She can't take the risk. Not now.

'If you ignore me again, I shall hang up,' I warn. 'Now take your finger out of your mouth.' I wait for a couple of seconds. 'Now, pick up the sheet and –'

'– and continue pulling down. I get it.'

'On the contrary, I want you to raise the sheet above you so you can look down underneath it. What do you see? Describe what you can see.'

'I see my tummy, bathed in shadows.'

'Good, anything else?'

'I see my thighs, rolling outwards, my feet hooked under the end of the sheet, hooked out the same way. And I see her. I see the hair around my pussy. If I dropped the sheet now I could touch her and you would never know.'

'Oh, I would know.'

V laughs. 'Yes, I think you would.'

'Now lower the sheet,' I tell her, 'and pull it down your body until only your bottom half is covered. Can you do that?'

'I've done it. I look like a sandcastle in the shape of two legs. Just an outline.'

'It's not just two legs, though, is it?'

'I can see my feet.'

'And what else?'

'Between my thighs there's a raised area. But it's not solid. It's hair.'

'Very lovely hair, if I recall. Very neat.'

'You're very kind. And what a memory.'

I smile. 'Tell me how it looks when you pull the sheet side to side there.'

'It's pretty. '

'That's nice. I want you to concentrate on just that area now as you move the sheet. Can you do that?'

'Yes.'

'Good. Keep pulling the sheet, and keep staring at

that soft bush. Now tell me, how does it feel?'

'Incredible. Like the rest of my body has shut down. Like every nerve ending I have is wired into that spot. That's weird, isn't it?'

'That's not weird. That's very good.'

I know she's enjoying this. I can picture her face as she talks to me. I hear her voice trail as she moves her head away from the phone to get a better view of her own body.

I love the way she derives as much pleasure from admiring her beauty and her curves as I do, as everyone does, as anyone would. She takes nothing for granted. Nothing is for show. When she runs her hand under her skirt and unhooks the clasps of her suspender belt, she knows it arouses her audience, but that's not why she does it. When she slides a hand along her thigh and under each side of her stocking, and inches the silk down her raised and outstretched leg, she knows it is enough to melt the iciest heart, but that is not why she does it. She is more lost in the sensation of the fabric against her skin than anyone watching could be. She knows, from experience, that the vision of her doing this can transfix any man, she knows that he'll be hers for the rest of the night. She knows this. She doesn't need to look. And she doesn't want to. She enjoys the view, she is a voyeur spying on her own erotic disrobing.

The biggest turn-on in the world is a partner who enjoys their body as much as you do. And V does. Every time. She physically delights in her own shape, in her own responses, in her own desires. She is as impressed by the sight of her breasts when they are released from her black balconette bra as any man.

Or woman.

But that's another story.

'Tell me what you want to do,' I ask her.

'I want to explore them,' she says. 'I want to reach down and part them, I want to bury my fingers among the hairs. Can I?'

From the inflection in her voice I know she wants to drop the sheet and reach down. She's not faking it. She never fakes anything. I can picture her eager hands desperate to plunge beneath the sheet, to answer the call of her lust, to quench the thirst of her pussy.

Should I let her?

'No, V, not yet,' I say.

There's a cry of adolescent petulance. Then a sound as she senses I have plans. As much as she wants to satisfy the building desire between her thighs, she wants to play more.

'Are your feet still covered by the sheet?' I ask.

'Yes.'

'Good. I want you to hook the cloth under one heel then pull it tight with the opposite hand.

Can you do that?'

'What do I do with the other hand?' she asks expectantly.

'What do you want to do with it?'

'I want to lick my fingers and slide them under the sheet,' she says. 'I want to push down on my pussy, I want to feel the heat and wetness that I know is there, I want to part my lips and dip my finger into the hotness. I want to bring them back out, back up to my clit, and spread my juice around my clit, dress my clit in my pussy juice, and massage it with a finger either side, pushing down and around in the silky wetness, not touching it directly, not yet.'

'I'd like you to do that,' I say. 'But not yet.'

'You're evil,' she says, but I hear her smile. The agony of suspense is killing her, but it's keeping her on edge as well. Knowing how much she wants to touch herself but can't is arousing both of us. But I have to be strong. I have work to do. I need to concentrate. She'll thank me for it later.

'What I want you to do with your spare hand,' I tell her, 'is to hold the phone properly. You keep drifting away. Now with your other hand, I want you to lift the sheet a few inches in the air and pull it tightly. You should have a line diagonally across your body, down to your foot.'

'I'm doing it. It looks like a white wall.'

'That's good. Now bend your toes forwards and feel the sheet tug in your hand.'

'I feel it.'

'Now pull back with your hand and feel your foot curl back the other way.'

'That's happening too.'

'Good. Keep doing that, very slowly, and gradually lower your hand, so the wall gets smaller and smaller and –'

'Oh God!'

Her cry is expected but her passion can never be predicted. Her responses where sex is concerned are pure animal reactions. Prick me and I bleed. Touch me and I scream. Fuck me and I come.

'Jesus, that feels nice,' she laughs.

'Keep moving the sheet, keep pulling it forwards and backwards, keep the rhythm steady, keep slowly lowering your hand.'

'Mmm,' she purrs, 'I'm not sure how much lower I can go. Oh, it's delicious, so soft.' She giggles. 'And so wet.'

'Tell me what you feel.'

'Mmm, I feel the sheet rubbing against me. I feel it pushing down on my *mons veneris*, my little mound, I feel it pushing my lips apart and sliding between them. Mmm. I don't think I can talk any more.'

'Yes, you can, I want to hear everything you feel.'

'Oh, you're so mean. OK, I'll try.'

I hear her take a deep breath. She's trying to take control. But her body has other ideas.

'If I move my foot a little, I can steer the sheet. I can make it drag across my nipple. I can make it rub up and down my breast. I can reach the sheet with my tongue. I can lick it and feel my own moisture rub down on to my nipple, and watch my body respond.'

'You're doing well.'

'I'm trying to be good for you. I can feel the sheet between my thighs. It's so soft, not like fingers, not like a tongue, not like lips. It's like a cotton feather being draped across me, trying to tickle me, to make me laugh. I'm not ticklish, not there. But it feels like I am. It's frustrating. I want it to stop. I don't want to be touched so lightly. I want the feather to press harder, I want to feel it push down, I want to feel it enter me.'

'But it can't, can it?'

'No, but I can try. I can push my hips up and pull the sheet down so tightly that it's against me. It's rubbing my pussy, it's touching all around her, pressing against her silky opening, pulling her apart with one movement and closing her with the next. Mmm, I want more. I need to feel more. I need to feel it inside me.'

'Tell me about your clitoris. Tell me how it feels when the sheet brushes past. Tell me how it responds when you let the cotton drag across its head.'

'Don't make me touch there, not yet.'

I smile again. She's getting into this. She wants the pain of frustration to end, but she needs the pleasure to go on and on. She wants to feel the sheet inside her pussy because that might make her explode. But she doesn't want to linger on her clit because that definitely will. No, she wants to drag this out. But I'm making the rules here. And I say we press on.

'V, dear, unless you do exactly what I say, I will have to hang up. Do you understand?'

She grunts. I think it means yes.

'Good, now tell me about your clitoris.'

'It feels big. It feels proud, like a soldier, tall, standing firm. But it feels soft too, as soft as the sheet, as wet as the sheet from my pussy. I can see it, sometimes. Sometimes the sheet is wrapped around it, sometimes it drops the other side. It looks like it's towelling down after a shower, like it's all refreshed. But it feels different, it has work to do. It feels like it's calling out, it wants attention, it wants me to pull the sheet against it more forcefully, to really nuzzle up to it, to bend it over if I can, to let it fight back, to resist the pressure, to resist the sheet and press against it. Mmm.'

'I know this is hard for you, but I want you to pull the sheet even more slowly now. I want you to pull one way for the count of five, then back for the count of five. No more, no less. I want to picture the gradual touch rising along your thigh, between your legs, up among your lovely hair. Then back again, nudging your clitoris, skimming your hair, releasing the tug on your pussy and again brushing against your leg. I want to picture all that, again and again.'

'I'm doing it, but it's too much. It's getting too much, it's so soft, I need more, I need to feel much more.'

'With your spare hand I want you to reach between your legs.'

'Under the sheet?'

'Oh no, V, not under the sheet. I want you to reach down and let your fingers run over the top of the cotton until they dip down between your legs. I want you to feel the heat from your pussy through the cloth. Linger there awhile until you feel the warmth. I want you to feel how damp it is. If you want, you can bring your fingers to your tongue to taste. You know what flavour it will be but you're still surprised when you lick, aren't you? It's nice, isn't it? But you must put them back. I want you to explore your pussy with your fingers. I want you to press down against the sheet and see how it feels to touch those familiar soft lips locked at the heart of your inner thigh, that small but welcoming opening that resists for a second but flowers with your nuzzling and lets you inside. And I want you to tell me how it feels. Your fingers are blindfolded, you have to describe everything to yourself.'

There is silence for a few seconds as she rests the phone once again against the pillow. I only hear her breathing. She tries to concentrate on balancing the phone but her body is distracting her, calling out to her, making her look back.

'I'm pushing my fingers in now,' she says. 'Two of them, inside the sheet. This is wonderful. I'm pushing, they're disappearing. Oh, I feel so full. I'm so wet, but the sheet is heavy, it's resisting, it's sticking to my walls, it won't go in.'

'Of course it will,' I assure her. 'You have to be patient. You have to push slowly, to let it soak against you.'

'It's pulling on my other hand. Oh, that's horny. The more my fingers go in, the tighter it pulls the rest of the sheet. Mmm, it feels bigger than two fingers. I'm squeezing them with my pussy. I'm eating them, pulling them in, trying to swallow them whole.'

'When you're as far in as you can go, I want you to pull your fingers out,' I tell her.

'It's too soon.'

'Trust me. I want you to remove your fingers, but leave the sheet where it is. Slide your fingers out, but let its sheath stay inside you. Pull your fingers out, but leave your cotton cock where it is, filling you, touching you, reaching inside you.'

'I'm doing it now. I'm squeezing so tightly the sheet isn't moving. But it's touching me everywhere at once. I know where my fingers are but when they move it feels like they're everywhere, touching all parts of me, rubbing everywhere at once, pushing against every point, caressing every millimetre.'

'Now I want you to use those same fingers and rest them on your clitoris. You can see it through the sheet, can't you? You can see it standing erect, surrounded by hair, at the top of your pussy, can't you? I want you to touch it, touch it with the same fingers that just pushed inside you. I want you to touch it as hard as you can bear, then put your fingers each side, and squeeze them together, squeeze them together so your clitoris is clamped. And I want you to pull your hand back, so your fingers rub against your clitoris, so they stimulate, and arouse, and pleasure.'

'Mmm, I'm doing it, I'm doing it for you. I'm running my fingers each side, through the sheet. Oh, this is too good. I don't know how long I can do this for. Mmm, too nice.'

I listen for a moment. It's nearly time. I'm nearly ready. I'm nearly finished with her.

'Not long now,' I tell her, and I hear her sigh with

pleasure and recognition. 'Keep playing with your clitoris, keep rubbing and smoothing and pressing against and running the sheet over. Start to get faster now, start to build up the pressure, build up the speed, let your hands fly as they touch you. I'm not counting now, I'm just listening to you. I'm just listening to you breathing. I'm listening to you making those noises that mean you're enjoying yourself. Those noises that mean you want to come. You do want to come, don't you?'

'Uh-huh.'

It's the most I can expect. I hear the rustling movement of her hand against the sheet and her head pushing down into the velvety bosom of the pillow. I hear her ear brushing against the receiver then turning away. She's tossing her head, left and right. Sitting up, then collapsing back down. She's lost to me. Every sinew of her body is arching towards her groin, every thought in her mind is focused on one thing. I sense she's on the edge. A few seconds, no more, from ecstasy.

'Pull the sheet,' I say. 'Pull it out of your pussy.'

I don't know if she hears me. I don't know if she pulls it. I don't know if the unexpected sensation as the sheet is withdrawn, the soft-touch massage of every fibre of her pussy, helps her explode with noise and pleasure.

But I hear her. I hear the release of her frustration, the unbottling of the morning's sexual tension. I hear her almost cry as the waves of orgasm reach out from her centre and take control of her whole body, washing down each leg, up each arm, around her neck, into her brain and out of her mouth.

She sounds close to sobbing, but it is the heaviness of her breathing, panting mixed with physical relief and laughter. I listen, staying quiet. London is awake now. She has woken everyone up.

'How are you feeling?' I ask her.

She giggles. 'Ooh, suddenly I'm feeling really hungry.'

'I think I can help you there.'

I put the phone down into its cradle, walk back into my kitchen and pick up the tray of breakfast I have prepared. I cross the lounge and open a door leading from the hallway. Inside the room V is on the bed, leaning on one elbow, the phone still on the pillow beside her. She radiates the cosmic glow that only one thing can trigger.

'That was amazing,' she says. 'Who says men can't multitask?'

III

V IS FOR VICTIM

'Are you awake?'

I love the way she texts. Never an abbreviation. Never a 'l8r' where 'later' will do. Never 'lol' to tell me she's laughing. Never a bracket to show she's sad.

'Are you awake?'

I love the way she uses text for conversation. She wants to engage. She wants feedback, answers, advice. She doesn't start a conversation with a statement. Not from her: 'I hate David. He's so dull.' What do you say to that? It's the textual equivalent of 'Talk to me, I'm bored. Ask me about David.'

'Ask me about me, Me, ME!'

She is never bored. And she never has to ask.

'Are you awake?'

That's a question. What she wants to say is important now. What she wants to ask has just occurred to her. She is of the moment. She responds to the immediate. She lives for each second. She is natural, open, honest. Responsive and reactive.

And she wants a conversation. With me.

'Are you awake?'

She asks questions all the time. She doesn't reveal anything. Not unless you ask like you care. And most people don't.

But she doesn't mind. She wants to communicate, to learn, to take on new information, new experiences. That is the most important thing to her. I've seen her do it so many times. I've seen rooms full of people bewitched, one after the other. Falling like dominos. They don't even realize it's happening. I've seen dozens of egos teased and inflated, one by one. A gathering of strangers, all struck dumb. All thinking she singled them out. All thinking they're the one she chose to talk to. That they had something that appealed to her, that won her over, that enticed her over to them.

A Mexican wave of smugness, of beatific warmth, follows her around the room. Her trail of Tinkerbell dust, of dazed smiles on the faces of strangers, gives her away. She can't hide. Not in a crowd. Not from me.

You can meet her a dozen times and learn nothing about her. You don't even realize. You're oblivious to the one-way traffic. You don't see your own reflection staring back when she laughs at your jokes, dazzles with her eyes, holds her finger just inside her lip, at the corner of her mouth, enrapt in your story, in your life, in you.

But I know about her. I know how she thinks. I know how she moves, how she dresses, how she talks. I know what makes her smile with her mouth and what makes her smile with her eyes. I know how to send an electric spark of excitement flashing across her face.

I know she can outrun Time. I know she can appear in two places at once. I know she is not what she seems.

I know what she wants. I know who she wants. I know what she needs. I know who she needs.

And more.

I know what makes her risk everything for the touch of a stranger, the illicit kiss of an unknown figure in the shadows. I know what makes her put her finger on a stranger's lips, and trace it down, onto his chin, then slowly underneath, lightly following the line of his stubble, across his Adam's apple and down, down into the V of his open shirt, resting where the first hairs of his chest brush against her. I know what makes her stare into his eyes, daring him to blink, to blush, to say 'no'.

I know what makes her smile and walk away. I know what makes her so sure that he'll be watching her exit through the dinner-suited guests at the charity ball. That he'll be following her with his stunned gaze. Then following with his feet, with his body, with his heart.

I know what she's thinking as she glides past the gathered friends, as she rests a hand on the shoulder of an important guest, as she smiles and converses but doesn't stop walking. I know what she's thinking as she catches the eye of one – two – three – more – of the wealthy strangers she ensnared earlier, as she sparkles in their direction, as she never stops moving.

I know what she's thinking when she reaches the edge of the room and emerges into the hotel corridor. I know she'll linger a second or two before moving on. I know she wants to be spotted. She wants to be seen turning left, walking towards the cloakrooms. She wants to confuse as she slows down to look around her. She wants to shock as she pushes the door marked 'Gentlemen' and enters.

I know she still hasn't looked back.

I know the door will open a second time. I know the man will stand there, in the entrance, not sure whether to proceed. He'll stare ahead at the woman carefully applying her lipstick in the mirror above the onyx sink. He'll think that it must be some kind of mistake. Some kind of joke. Some kind of trap. He doesn't know this woman. He knows who she is – Christ, everyone in the hotel knows who she is. But he's never met her before tonight. He's never even spoken to her. She suddenly appeared in front of him, looked into his eyes, and . . .

And now he's standing in the gents' toilet watching her touch up her make-up.

He thinks about leaving. It must be a hoax. Something is wrong. She's ignoring him. He imagined it. What was he thinking? She's the wife of the host. What was he thinking?

He reaches out for the door handle.

'Going so soon?' she whispers.

He hasn't heard her speak before. Not in the flesh. Only through a microphone. Only accepting a cheque on behalf of her husband's chosen charity. Only as she thanked everyone for coming tonight and for giving so generously.

A noise comes from inside one of the gold-lined cubicles. 'Who's there?' a voice calls out. 'I think you'll find the ladies' are next door, my dear.'

She smiles and points to the cubicle. She wants him to speak. But he can't think of what to say. He can't think of anything. He can't remember how to work his tongue. He opens his mouth but nothing comes out.

She gestures again towards the cubicle.

He coughs and opens and closes the door behind him. 'It's OK, old chap, she's gone now,' he calls out and delights as she mimes a round of applause.

'Very good,' she mouths. 'You're very good.'

Is he blushing? Has he ever blushed before? He suddenly feels like he's in a sauna, like the temperature has been raised around him, like he's about to be offered a hot towel to wrap around his tense body.

She moves silently away from the mirror and towards the row of cubicles. The first shows 'engaged'; three others are vacant. She chooses the end door, pushes and disappears from view.

He waits. He waits for a second too long. The first cubicle is unlocked and the door begins to open. In two long strides he reaches the far booth and enters. He barely hears the other man say, 'Funny that girl finding her way in here, don't you think?'

He barely hears his own grunted reply. He barely hears anything above the sound of his own frantic pulse. Above the sound of his own breathing.

He leans back on the closed door, half aware of the sound of running water outside, and then of the main door swinging open and falling shut.

He's safe.

But safe from what? Safe from being discovered in a toilet with the wife of an aristocrat? The wife of one of the non-execs on his company board? A woman who must surely come to her senses at any moment, who must be seconds away from snapping out of her alcohol-fuelled fantasy, who must realize how out of place she seems in even this overly grand booth.

A woman who must look at him and see a mistake about to happen, who must want to scream, 'Help!'

But she doesn't look like that. He can see in her eyes that she wants to be there. He can see in her smile as she leans closer that she's not about to do anything but kiss. And he can tell from the taste of her tongue as it licks slowly across his bottom lip that not a drop of the freely available champagne has left her glass.

This is a woman who knows what she is doing.

This is a woman who knows what she is doing as she pushes him back against the black leather-clad door and puts one hand behind his head, to run her nails down the nape of his neck and under his loose collar, to sink into his firm, defined shoulders, to pull him closer. This is a woman who knows exactly what she is doing as she presses against his chest, her head tilted upwards to force her mouth onto his, her lips onto his, her tongue against his.

Any thought of fear has vanished. His hands, so recently hanging uselessly by his sides, reach out and feel the heat of her hips as she leans into his groin. With each urgent kiss, he feels her grind forwards into him, wanting to get closer, wanting to enter him, wanting them to become one.

'Ouch!'

The pain is sudden and exquisite. He touches a finger to his lip and stares.

'I'm bleeding,' he says. 'You bit me.'

She looks up at him with large, brown eyes. Her words are contrite – 'I'm sorry,' she says – but her eyes are aroused. Do they reflect the overhead lights or are they wild with excitement? She wants to bite him all over. She wants to scratch him. She wants to make him choke on his own gasps as she leaves her mark on this unknown body.

'Am I too rough?' she asks with eyebrows raised in concern.

But he knows she doesn't care about the answer. And what would he say anyway?

Stepping back slightly, she reaches both hands inside his shirt and under his collar. There's a rip as she jerks both hands down and three buttons scatter on the floor like hail on corrugated iron.

'Oops,' she says. 'Clumsy me.'

He doesn't care. He doesn't care about the shirt. He doesn't care about the ferocity with which she moves her head against his exposed chest and takes a mouthful of hair and skin between her teeth and pulls. He doesn't care as she slides her hands around his waist and violently rips until the remaining buttons ping across the marble tiles. He doesn't care as she digs the talons of both hands into the small of his back and draws them round the sensitive flesh of the sides of his waist till they meet, then steps back to admire the nail-print cummerbund she's etched into his skin.

'That's better,' she murmurs. 'Dress codes must be observed.'

He tries to take the initiative. He forces his weight forwards and she steps back towards the toilet seat. The stall is roomy but by no means big. For a second she lets him position her – then, as her calf touches the porcelain behind her, with unexpected fury she pushes him back against the door, the air expelled suddenly from his anxious lungs as his full weight crashes to a halt against the unyielding leather.

The noise echoes around the ornately tiled bathroom like thunder in a church, and they both freeze.

She cocks her head to listen for newcomers arriving. He winces and tries to catch his breath.

What has he let himself in for?

Who is this woman?

What does she want?

Certain (but relieved or not? He can't tell) that no one has arrived to investigate the disturbance, she looks back at him and with another sudden movement latches her hand around the fastener on his belt. There's a click and he feels his back lurch forwards and a rapid burning sensation on one hip as she reels the leather strap from around him.

'This is mine now,' she says, trailing the belt from

her hand like a snake charmer clutching a cobra's throat.

Holding the metal clasp with her right hand, she pulls the leather across her open left palm. He watches, intrigued, intoxicated and insecure, as with eyes closed she bites her own lip and murmurs.

'Mmm.'

It's distinct and erotic. The insecurity in his body vanishes. He is suddenly only aware of lust. Of wanting her to touch him again, to etch her mark on to his skin, to draw blood from his flesh, to press powerfully into the hardness growing in his loosened trousers.

But he dare not move. He remains pinned to the leather door, a target for her knife throwing. He smiles at the thought. If she had a knife, he's convinced she would use it. Luckily she doesn't have a knife.

But she does have the belt.

Ftisssh!

The leather whiplashes against the upholstered door, inches from his face. He winces.

Ftisssh!

This time it lands the other side. She's getting her range, he thinks. She doesn't want to hurt me.

Wrong.

Ftisssh!

With the sharp smack of an electric shock, the belt rasps across his exposed chest and is gathered up again.

Ftisssh!

Again, the same spot. He feels weak. The blood is draining from his face. The pain is like nothing he has ever felt. It's excruciating and savage yet accurate and almost scientific at the same time. In her hands the belt is a scalpel, an instrument of precision.

She coils the leather around her left hand, like a lasso, and walks over to him. Placing her other hand on his shoulder, she bends to examine the welts left by the lashes. 'Very nice,' she purrs. 'Very nice.'

He is distracted from the pain momentarily as she licks the length of his overheated, pulsating neck. But as her tongue next runs along the small cuts made by the belt, and the salt from her mouth reacts angrily with his exposed skin, he wonders: was she intentionally gathering perspiration from his neck? Was she intentionally trying to arouse him and hurt him at the same time? To hurt him with his own salt, with his own sweat, with his own body? The answer, he understands, is yes.

This woman has ways of inflicting pain that he hasn't even dreamed of. But it's not pain that he has ever known, either. It's not pain as he has felt it in the past. It's not the physical agony he has experienced before.

He has never felt so out of control in his life. He is in a men's lavatory with a beautiful socialite. This

63

is something like a dream. He should be calling the shots. He should be in charge.

But he is in pain.

And he is in no doubt that the pain could get worse and there is nothing he can do about it.

She approaches him, beckons him to bow his head forwards slightly, and drapes the belt around his shoulders, like an undone tie. Then she reaches down and, without looking, slips her hand inside his trousers.

Any semblance of pain vanishes at that moment.

'I was looking forward to meeting you,' she whispers. But he knows she's not talking to him. At least, not to all of him. Finally she looks down and carefully unzips his trousers. Working quickly she thrusts her hand inside the fly and pulls out his cock.

'Somebody's been having fun, haven't they,' she says, and traces her finger around its head, massaging the tip of the penis in its own released juice.

He groans as she pushes back his foreskin with one hand, as though she were carefully preparing an exotic fruit, peeling back its cover for the sweetness within. He feels her fingers slide down his shaft, then her palm as her wrist nuzzles against the head. She grasps the shaft firmly and he feels an involuntary spasm press against the inside of her wrist.

'Oh, that's nice,' he says, but she is silent. Has she even heard him? Still standing, she drops her shoulder slightly, causing her hand to fall lower and force more pressure down on his straining foreskin. As she squeezes, he feels his balls start to tighten. Pleasure overwhelms him. The pleasure of anticipation, of having this decadent stranger experiment carnally on his body, of having his penis caressed by the soft yet powerful hands of this amazingly experienced temptress.

If he could think about anything apart from the thumb and fingers stretching down to his balls, he might realize that he has only been in the cubicle for five minutes, although it feels like so much longer. If he could concentrate on anything apart from the delicate probing of her other hand up his shaft, he might have worried that another stranger could walk into the room at any moment and his dream would end. That the stranger might call security. That he might call his boss. That he might lose everything if discovered exposed and half naked?

If he could concentrate he might consider many things.

All he can think about is the painted nail of her right hand that she places underneath the head of his cock, and presses. He knows it must hurt, but he can't feel it. He knows she could draw blood, but he can't stop her. He knows she could damage him forever if he doesn't stop her, but he can't imagine the future. He can only think of now. He can only think of the unknown buzz of pleasure surging from his cock to all corners of his body, and back again. He feels invigorated, electrically charged, and ready for anything.

She looks up and kisses him. Softly at first, then more urgently again. She releases his cock and pulls on each end of the draped belt, until his head cowers to meet hers. Breathing heavily to match his own panting gasps for air, she pulls his forehead against hers. Her hair falls forwards and over both their faces, but he can see she is staring intensely into his eyes. The pressure of the belt cuts into the back of his neck. He couldn't move if he wanted to.

'My turn,' she says.

Wrapping her arms around the back of his neck, he freezes as she elevates one leg to waist height and wraps it around his hip. The power takes his breath away briefly. He looks at her, this ballerina standing perfectly on one leg before him, coiling her limbs around him, constricting his breath. With a sudden movement she pulls harder on his neck and her standing leg grips around him too. He staggers forwards, but catches himself and falls once more back against the door. She isn't heavy at all, for all her five-foot-ten frame, but the move caught him by surprise.

He feels pressure all over his body as she steadies herself and locks her feet behind him, each movement forcing more air from his lungs, weakening him, weakening his will, weakening his energy to fight her off.

He is an onlooker in his own body as she pulls herself on him, moving minutely to get comfortable.

But she is not getting comfortable, he realizes. She is not struggling to keep her balance.

With each manoeuvre against his hip, she presses herself into him and moves away, presses again, and moves.

She is getting off on him. Literally.

He hears her breathing change. Her mouth is by his ear now. She nuzzles his lobe with her nose, then nibbles, all the time exhaling hot noisy air against his face. 'Fuck me now,' she growls. 'Just fuck me.'

He realizes that she is as immaculately dressed now as she was when he followed her out of the main hall. Her thigh-length cocktail dress pulls taut against the top of her thighs, and he can't get his hand between fabric and skin. But underneath is a different story. Running both hands at once along the underside of her legs, he feels the cloth end and her skin begin. He is shocked. It is so cool. The arms clamped around his neck are as hot as her face. The heat from her chest pressed against his could melt ice. And yet her thighs and her peachy soft arse are so cool.

At first he assumes she is not wearing panties, but his fingers run up against a fine line of silk, stretched unnaturally tight by the angle of her open legs. He hooks a thumb underneath the constricting cloth and traces down, round past the perfect curve of her cheek, round and down to where a fine base of hairs appears, where the temperature increases with his touch. One more inch, he knows, is all he needs to move. One more inch.

He knows he can move that inch with his hand. Or, he can use that hand to pull aside the thin material.

He bends his legs slightly, feels her weight shift around his neck, and with his spare hand guides his cock up against the inside of her thigh, against the hot silk being pulled back, and finally – finally – against the smooth welcoming heat of her pussy.

He straightens and with that motion his world goes dark.

Time has stopped.

He is asleep. He is awake. He is dead. He is alive. He can feel nothing. He can feel every nerve in his body screaming in ecstasy. All at once. All at the same time.

His eyes have been open all along but suddenly he can see again.

He sees her hair, matted over his face. Her face is next to his, her cheek pressed against his, the vice of her arms pulling her head against his.

'Oh, yes,' she says. 'Oh, yes. Give it to me.'

Using his arms to lever her weight, he bends his legs slightly and feels the terrible vacuum as his cock slides out of her pussy. It's the last thing he wants. He could happily die inside her. But still he withdraws. Still he pulls away. He's nearly out. But not quite. He keeps the tip inside.

'Do it,' she orders.

He releases his grip on her thighs and lets gravity take her plunging down on to his cock with a powerful thrust. His balls shudder at the impact, he feels engulfed, dominated by the molten grip that holds his shaft. Again he lifts her, and again she falls. With each descent, she clings tighter around his neck, with each plummet he straightens harder to push his cock up into her.

Again and again. Harder and harder. Deeper and deeper. She doesn't move, but she works his cock expertly. There is no technique, there are no tricks, no moves at work. It is passionate, they are passionate. They are animals, locked together, pounding each other with their bodies. They don't kiss, they don't speak, they just cling to each other and let motion take control. He straightens, he bends. She rises, she falls. He forces his way into her pussy, she repels him then demands him back.

Again and again. Harder and harder. Deeper and deeper.

He is beginning to tire. With each bend of his leg it is harder to straighten. He wants to turn round, to press her back against the leather door, to use his weight to keep her aloft, to let science carry them on.

Without altering his momentum he starts to turn but she slams a hand against the thin cubicle partition.

'No,' she hisses. 'No.' She is beginning to strangle him with her neck hold. But he can't stop now.

Again and again. Harder and harder. Deeper and deeper.

Just as he feels the numbness of surrender attack his thigh muscles, she moves. She releases her bear hug around his shoulders and leans backwards.

'Yes,' she says. Then, louder, 'Oh, yes!'

As she stretches away from him, her legs lock tighter around his waist, punishing his lungs, forcing his breathing to become urgent and desperate, but he can't think about that now.

When he can barely support them any more, she reaches forwards and grabs the ends of the belt around his neck. The sudden pull on his nape leaves a burn. He winces but the pain passes. The new position is all-consuming. She puts her feet against the door and somehow raises herself using the belt for balance. She's four foot off the floor and she's able to push herself up and down.

Up and down.

On his cock.

He hears a tear as the toe of her mule pushes through the leather door cover. She doesn't notice. She pushes off again, pulling against his neck once more, and he feels his rider threaten to dismount, standing up in her stirrups, then drop her weight back down on him, crashing down into the saddle, on to him.

He's not bucking any more. She's doing the work. It's all he can do to stand up. The burning on his neck is getting intense, the desire to let his head drop forwards and watch the belt slide over his head and end the pain is immense. But he fights it. He keeps his head upright, he keeps the belt searing into his naked skin, he keeps his legs locked as she rides him, as he becomes her childhood love, her earliest fantasy.

A noise. It's the door. Someone is in the bathroom. They should stop. But she hasn't heard.

She doesn't hear the noise they make as her shoe splits the leather further. She doesn't hear each thrust force his weight crashing back against the cushioned door. She doesn't hear him groaning with exhaustion, with pain, with the arrival of orgasm.

Or does she?

He is about to crumble, his legs are about to buckle when she mouths silently: 'I'm coming.'

From nowhere he has the strength of ten men. If he is suffering, he has forgotten how or where. The burning on his neck is nothing compared to the steam bath of his cock as she glides up and down. He feels only her pleasure, the heightened grip as she nears climax.

It wasn't intentional, he isn't that skilled. But they come together. Her pleasure triggers a key in his head. As he watches her rock back suddenly, her mouth open in a silent scream, he realizes that he cannot stop the rushing in his own body, the complete rush of all his senses as his cock explodes inside her. He feels his body spasm and each movement grows more intense.

Again and again. Harder and harder. Deeper and deeper.

He feels his pulsing hardness now alert to new sensations. Her pussy seems different to him now. Still as hot, but coated with him. Still as tight, but familiar and friendly. Still wrapped around him but comfortably now, without the exhaustion of thrusting.

They rest together, locked. He leans back against the door trying to support them. His eyes are closed. He doesn't see her look around as though waking after deep sleep. He doesn't see her smile as she tightens her grip on the belt and pulls herself up.

As she gets closer to him, his legs can take no more and as he slides down the door, her feet drop to the floor and she lands stealthily, suddenly disengaged from his body. He is sitting on the floor, shirt open like a jacket, red mounds pocking his rapidly rising and falling chest. She is standing over him like a colossus, the victor in a wrestling match towering over her vanquished foe.

She bends down and kisses the top of his head.

'Thanks,' she says.

Without saying anything else, she straightens her dress and gestures towards the door. He leans to one side and she is able to pull the door enough for her to squeeze out.

He doesn't know if the other man is still in the bathroom. He doesn't know if she cleans herself at the mirror, if she can salvage a suitable look for a dinner crowd from the radiant lover who leaves him now. He doesn't know if she gets out of the bathroom without being seen by the staff or the other guests or her husband.

He doesn't know whether his wounds will heal. He doesn't know whether he can find all his buttons.

He doesn't know what the hell just happened to him. But as he leans back against the door, and lets his head sink into the ravaged leather, he smiles and closes his eyes. He doesn't know that in four hours' time he will be awoken by a hotel cleaner. He doesn't know that his night with the society queen will never be repeated. He doesn't know anything except that he must sleep.

'Are you awake?'

The glinting text won't go away. Yes, I'm awake. I'm awake now. But I wasn't when she sent the message. I'm awake and frustrated.

There's no point replying. The moment has gone. I know her thoughts will be a hundred miles away now. I know her mood will have passed. I know she'll have found another to talk to, someone else whose morning she can brighten.

IV

V IS FOR VIRTUAL

V always gets the best tables. She gets the best of everything. And not by asking. People like her, even if they've never met, even before she's opened her mouth. It's an instinctive thing. You know how some people exude menace? You can't put your finger on it, but you know they're best avoided? It's like that with her, but in reverse. Her aura hits your brain before she says anything, before she does anything. On some sort of feral level you want to please her.

And she wants to please you.

I've got used to the nods from the doormen whenever we eat anywhere grand enough to employ them. I've got used to the way staff appear from nowhere to remove her coat, take her bag, offer their personal best wishes for the evening. It's like they want to touch her, to speak to her, to make an impression on her. They all want to be remembered.

And she does remember.

I've even got used to the occasional flash of a photographer's bulb as we step out of the cab.

The paparazzi who hang around these restaurants know her pictures won't sell to the tabloids and gossip magazines, but they take them anyway. They want to capture her image for themselves. And, of course, they want to chat.

The society pages run her photo as often as they can, but her name is unknown to the majority, to the masses who don't follow big business or the goings-on of the silver spoon brigade. Her husband is more familiar to the media than she is. But she is the reason they photograph him. It's good for his image. It's good for his business.

I wonder sometimes whether V would behave differently if she were more famous. Would she take so many risks? Would she behave so naturally? Would she be so utterly ruled by the free spirit that dominates her thinking?

So I ask her tonight, at dinner.

'You have to be true to yourself,' she says. 'You have to be honest.'

'That's rich, coming from someone with as many secrets as you have,' I laugh.

'But they're only secrets from other people. I don't keep anything from myself. How many men do you know who con themselves that they're something they're not? How many women are so desperate to make their marriage or their job or their friendships work that they lie to themselves about why they do it? About who they are? I know who I am. My husband knows who I am. You know who I am.'

'What about Clarisse and Michael?' I ask. 'Do they know who you are?'

'Who can tell?' she laughs. 'But they'll be here in about an hour. You can ask them.'

'An hour?'

'Clarisse rang me. They're running late.'

'Work problems, do you think?' I ask.

'I sincerely hope not.' V looks affronted. 'There is only one acceptable excuse for standing me up.'

'And that is?' Although I think I know the answer.

'Sex.'

I am right. It's a safe bet with V, but her reasons intrigue me.

'Sex before you go out is one of the greatest gifts society has given us,' she says. 'I know that's when I feel like it. You spend two hours getting ready, two hours arranging your body into its most perfectly presentable and, let's be honest, alluring arrangement, and then when you've finished your creation, you turn, you see your partner, and they've done the same. When do you normally look this good? You go to all this effort to appear A-grade fuckable, and for who? You'll never look hotter all night than at that moment, and normally the only people to see it are the concierge and your driver.'

'Do you really think that's what's keeping Clarisse and Michael?' I ask.

'I hope so. It would keep me. I think they're both beautiful.'

'Do you ever talk to Clarisse about what they do?'

'Of course! And you and Michael?'

'Never. Men don't. Not in any detail. Not about their partners. It's enough to let everyone know they're doing something. Regularly. And well, of course.'

'I dreamed about Michael last week. He came to the house for a meeting with LH.'

'And what happened next?'

'Nothing, annoyingly. It was very boring. They had a meeting and my imagination moved on to something else. But I thought about it a lot when I woke up. In fact, I forced myself to have the dream again, but this time I was in control. This time he came to the house, but it wasn't to see LH.'

'Do you want to tell me about it?'

'Well, I suppose we do have some time. Let me see . . .

I had just stepped out of the shower when Jacinta, my maid, told me he had arrived. I wrapped my hair in a towel and put on a soft dressing gown. By the time I reached the sitting room he was already there, looking out of the window. He didn't hear my bare feet pad across the deep carpet, which meant I got a good look at him from behind. It's not a view one normally sees. Not of a friend so engrossed in something else, standing so still, so stationary, so statue-like. He looked so proud, so perfectly sculpted. His suit was cut very flatteringly. It tapered at his waist, then bloomed at his shoulders. He seemed so powerful, so majestic standing there that I was overwhelmed with the urge to touch him. I wanted to feel his granite features with my fingertips, I wanted to press my face against the concrete of his chest and feel the marble of his face as he brought his lips down to mine.

Stealthily edging closer, I unwrapped the towel from my head and wound it around both wrists. I was so close to him now that I was sure he could hear my pounding heart, but he remained steadfast. I raised my hands and swiftly looped the towel over his head, covering his eyes and ears.

He didn't flinch.

Was he really a statue? Was he carved of ice?

I pulled back on the towel like a rider halting a stallion and his head barely moved. The powerful neck muscles visible above his collar trembled, but that was the only clue that my captive steed was alive. The only sign that there was blood in his body.

I tied a large knot in the towel and released my hands. It was a clumsy, giant blindfold but it served a purpose. For now. The dampness from my wet hair was beginning to leak down his back.

Placing a hand on each of his broad shoulders I took a breath and leaped. I actually mounted him. Instinctively his arms flinched and locked my legs tight against his hips. He was not a statue. He was a machine.

Adjusting my height I reached over his shoulder and pulled the knot of his tie until it began to loosen. There was enough space for me to slide my hand under his shirt. I fanned my fingers among his chest hair. It was wire to my touch.

'You're my horsey,' I whispered in his ear. 'Are you going to give me a ride?' Before he could answer I yelled, 'Giddy up!' and kicked my heels into the softness of his waist. I actually felt the breath expelled from his lungs as he was overcome by pain.

But he recovered.

'I'm not anyone's horsey,' he growled. 'But you are going to ride me.'

He moved so quickly I thought I was falling. But I wasn't. I was being lifted by this powerhouse, swung effortlessly by him from his back to his front. He was still wearing the towel, but we were face to face. He didn't look out of breath at all. He was in perfect show condition. But he would decide what he showed.

I've never felt such power in another human being. The grip I had round his neck was like cuddling a lamppost. My feet resting on his hips could have been on a mountain ledge. But his arms exposed his true strength.

Chunky fingers clamped my waist and I felt myself held aloft like a child. His grip was excruciating, it felt like my ribs would pop under the pressure. He held me like that for a couple of seconds, then took one step forwards. I heard a crash under his foot as a vase gave way, but he didn't stop moving. Even in darkness, he knew exactly where he was going.

When he released my weight, I felt the cold glass of the window through the back of my gown before my bottom landed on the cool wood of the large sill. With a careless hand I swept the area clear of the photographs he must have been admiring before I arrived. The last thing I wanted was an arse full of glass. But I don't know if he would have cared. He didn't waste any time. As soon as I'd been placed down, his hands were pulling at his trousers, undoing his fly. One hand disappeared from view for a second then emerged holding his cock, his beautiful, mesmerizing, fucking huge cock.

I don't know how long it was, but I've never seen anything thicker. I couldn't take my eyes off it. What the hell was he going to do with that thing?

I soon found out.

He took one step forwards, bent slightly, and fed his cock underneath the bottom of my gown. I couldn't wait for him to feel his way. I had to help. I needed that fat fucker inside me now.

I pulled my weight forwards and felt his hand against my groin. I went to put my hand there to guide him in, but I was too late. He had the tip of his cock against me, pushing, nuzzling, knocking on the door. Some of it was in the right place but some of it was missing. It was that wide. But I wasn't allowed to help.

Christ, it hurt as he went in. I felt ripped apart. It was so rough. I was on fire. He went in and it felt like I was being sucked in as well. I can't explain it. I knew I was wet, I knew I was ready, but not for him. This was something else. It was brutal, immediate, savage. And it was so fucking big.

I must have screamed because he stopped moving. He didn't say anything, but there was a definite pause. In a strange way it was worse. I could feel my pussy being stretched. The stillness accentuated the individual strains pulling on my flesh. I don't think I've been wetter, but at that moment it wasn't enough.

And then he started to move. Slowly at first so

I acclimatized to the girth. Then faster, and rougher. Short, jabbing thrusts that punished my poor, greedy pussy. Pneumatic pump actions that felt like violations and invitations at the same time.

It was rapid and it was furious and the feelings of pain and ecstasy swilled messily in my mind. And then it was over.

I came like a madwoman. He came like a bull. He was an angry lover and inconsiderate. But he was what I'd asked for. He was what I needed then.

'What do you think?' she asks when she's finished.

'That's a pretty good dream,' I say. 'I liked it.'

'I wonder how much . . .'

A second later I feel her stockinged foot brush against the inside of my thigh. It takes me by surprise but I soon recover my composure. She shifts in her seat and her leg extends by a few more inches. A few crucial inches.

'Oh, you did like it, didn't you? You like to think of me and Michael doing it. Is this why you're so hard?'

I nod. It's all I can do. She's pressed 'pause' and all I can think about is 'fast forward'. We compromise. She wants to 'play'.

The restraining cloth of my trousers and shorts holds my anxious cock still, totally restricting its movement, totally exposing it like a human sacrifice on an altar to the tantalizing probing of V's foot. I want to help, to release it, but I know if my hands leave the table the game is over. I can't move as she flicks her big toe up and down, easing my foreskin back, rubbing the head, sliding her nail along the engorged ridge, and releasing the pressure, letting my skin work up again, naturally constricting, naturally arousing, naturally wanking myself. My cock is tightly bound, it can't escape as she digs her toe lower down. She finds the main vein and presses, cutting off the blood supply for a few seconds. I feel my balls rise and tighten, and my head swell to what seems like double its size. I can picture what it looks like, shiny, eager and craving attention. But I can't reach down, I can't stroke it, comfort it. I'm in V's hands now. In the power of her feet. Working to her agenda.

'Do you ever think about Clarisse?' she asks me.

'I think she's lovely,' I'm just about able to splutter. But lovely or not, my thoughts are not with Clarisse. They're with the heel being rested at the base of my shaft, massaging my balls out of the way. Pushing them aside, squeezing them apart as far as they will go. They're with the foot running up the full length of my cock, pressuring it at intervals with her instep. They're with the toes she manages to curl over the top of my head, pressing down on the centre of my pleasure, of my concentration. Her foot rooted between my legs, she swings it in slight metronomic movements: left, right, tick, tock. They're subtle. The rest of her body stays still. No one would know what activity was going on below table level.

But I know. I can feel the windscreen-wiper motion of her dainty yet firm foot pressing me one way, pulling me the other, generating fireworks in my groin and a *son et lumière* experience in my mind. I can feel her dragging my cock down as far as the cloth will let it bend, then bolstering its height with upward jerking sweeps. I'm delirious with pleasure. The fact that every member of the waiting staff seems fixed on our table, and that another ninety customers dine obliviously nearby, just increases my sense of desperation. I need her to finish what she's started. I need to come.

'Tell me what you think about Clarisse,' she continues. 'Tell me what you dream about her. Tell me what you'd like to do to her when Michael's away on one of his business trips. Tell me how dirty you want to be with her.'

I admit I do think about Clarisse. What man wouldn't? She is a classic beauty, with long blonde hair, a pixie-pretty face and that rare figure clothes designers must have in mind when they market their creations. Most women struggle to find their 'size'; everything fits Clarisse. Everything was made for her.

'What do I get if I tell you my Clarisse fantasies?' I ask.

'What would you like?'

'I think you know that.'

'Well, let's see what we can do, shall we? Off you go. Your story please . . .'

It's very simple. I was staying in a hotel. I had been working. It was a summer's night and I was sticky with sweat. I was naked in bed and the thin sheet I'd been hiding under had long been kicked off. And then I started to dream. I dreamed that I was having sex. I dreamed that I'd muddled my keys up and walked in on a stranger touching herself in the room next door. She didn't look flustered — not by my presence anyway. Her pink cheeks were her own work.

She beckoned me over and I went. As soon as I got close enough she clamped her hands around my face and gave me the deepest, most passionate kiss I've ever experienced. At first it was just lips, just these amazing cushions. But then it was her tongue. It was so long. I was being forced back by her probing, but her hands pulled me towards her. She was gagging me with her tongue, I felt claustrophobic, I was struggling to breathe.

Suddenly she stopped. She dropped to her knees and pulled my trousers down. My cock sprang up towards her face like it was on a spring. She liked it. It was the only time I heard her voice but I couldn't make out what she said.

And then she fell on it, with the same passion that she'd shown in her kiss. It was like she wanted to punish me, to hurt me. She gripped so hard and wanked me so viciously that I thought she was trying to rip it off.

But she knew what she was doing. She knew how it would feel so much sweeter when she suddenly let go with her hands and caught me in her mouth. God, that girl could suck. I didn't feel her tongue, just her lips, locked on to my cock as hard as any handgrip, pulling me off with just her mouth alone. It was incredible. Visceral, animal contact being made. Instincts taking over from words. A total understanding between us.

But it was just a dream. I woke up and she wasn't there. But I was still hard. And I was still being sucked. I looked down and it wasn't the stranger. It was someone else, someone more familiar to me.

It was Clarisse.

I don't know when she came into my room, but she must have seen how aroused I was in my sleep. And she decided to do something about it.

Where the stranger's touch had been harsh, Clarisse's was smooth. Where my fantasy woman had wanted to consume me, Clarisse just wanted to taste, to swill me around in her mouth like a wine connoisseur, to luxuriate in the sensations on her tongue and the responses she could provoke. I don't know if the dream had been too real or whether Clarisse was too good, but I felt myself approach the point of no return. Part of me wanted to fight it, to savour the moment longer. But the other part of me wanted nothing on Earth more at that moment. Do it, Clarisse, I thought. Get rough with me, make me come.

Did she read my mind? Suddenly she stopped, somehow sensing how close I was. And instead of getting firmer, she loosened the grip of her lips, reduced the ferocity of her tongue flickers over my silky tip.

I wanted to buck into her face, to thrust myself against her. But I knew she would withdraw. I had to let her continue at her own pace. But it was not easy.

She was a feather flicking at my hardness, and her touch just got lighter and lighter, softer and softer.

I propped my head up with my arms to watch her work. She said nothing and neither did I. But her kisses were more gentle now, almost whispers. I felt the warmth of her breath more than her touch.

'This is driving me mad,' I thought. 'If she carries on like this she won't be touching me at all.'

I could see my cock twitching with expectation, sudden little spasms of energy that didn't feel like they came from me. But even though she was just millimetres above, she wasn't touching me. She was just blowing, just trying to stimulate me with air. And it worked.

'Any moment now she will have to touch me again,' I thought. And I was right. But it wasn't with her hands or her mouth.

Tossing her head to one side, Clarisse swung over a giant brush of beautiful blonde hair that landed like a golden carpet at the top of my thighs. Turning her face slightly, she dragged the hair up my body, over that sensitive area at the top of my legs. It was like being swept by angels. Individual hairs triggered off mini flickers of light in my skin, tiny sparks of energy that burst into life as she draped her silken locks slowly along.

When her hair reached my cock, I thought I would die. I expected it to tickle. But it felt like a bath of air. The strands fell everywhere, filling all sorts of spaces, reaching every part of my primed penis. Every minuscule nerve ending in my cock had an individual stimulant pressing almost imperceptibly against it. It felt like the most intense and yet the most invisible session of acupuncture. From my balls up to the tip, nothing was missed.

When she got to the top, she flicked her head the other way and swept back down. Then she did it again and again, but each time picking up a little speed, so the silken whispers became mini whiplashes. The massaging tentacles became more steely, and I felt their touch in my most sensitive parts.

I have never been flagellated so gracefully. Her hair fell on me again and again with almost no weight behind it, but it was enough. It was enough to summon all the pent-up energy she had caused minutes earlier with her tongue. It was enough to send my cock thrashing against my own stomach with its own powerful pulsing, as a stream of emotional and physical release arced out of me, and into Clarisse's hair. One, two, three separate streams fired up, and she didn't stop the calm brushing. Only when she was sure I'd stopped moving, when she was certain there was no more to come, did she lower her mouth back down again, and take my cock fully inside her mouth. As she pulled away, she kissed the tip and looked at me for the first time. As she turned, her features started to blur. The more I looked, the less focus I had, the less definition I could make out. It was no longer Clarisse's face. It was the stranger's. But I know it was Clarisse's hair, her tongue and her touch. I will always know it.

'I had no idea you felt that way,' V says. 'That's very interesting. Do you think you'll ever tell her?'

'I don't think it will ever come up.'

'Unlike our little friend down there,' she smiles. 'He's been up too long already. Past his bedtime, I think.'

'Stop toying with me, V,' I urge. 'I think I'm begging you. Either take your foot away or finish me off.'

'Which would you prefer?' She's sure of the answer. She's so sure, I'm desperate to prove her wrong.

'Take your foot away. If I come it will spoil my suit.'

'Really?' She's genuinely shocked. That is not the reason she expects. Disappointment creeps slowly over her face.

I feel her foot leave its comfort zone beneath my thighs. I feel her heel lift from the edge of the seat. I watch her adjust her balance and bring her foot back in. And then I act.

I don't know how quickly my hands move but the champagne flute knocked flying gives my game away. No matter. I now have two hands around V's ankle. I have her beautiful foot cradled in my hands. I have her poised inches above my cock. I have her ready to do my bidding.

The waiters have other ideas. They fuss around mopping up and replacing my drink, but I don't see them. I don't hear their apologies for what was my mistake, I just see V talking to one of them as though nothing else was going on in the rest of the world. As though no one was resting her foot on his cock in public; as though no one was trying to bury her foot inside his trousers, so desperate to create the friction necessary to get him off. To get him going. To get him to come.

I'm close now. Very close. I think I've stopped caring who sees me. Who notices the sweat appearing on my brow. Who spots both my hands in my lap, underneath my serviette, below the hem of the tablecloth. I'm in a world of my own. A world of pleasure, brought about by V.

I'm so close. A couple of seconds. Perhaps five, maybe four, maybe three. So very, very close. And then –

Fuck!

An interruption.

The *maître d'* is standing next to V. He is gesturing towards the entrance, where I see Michael and Clarisse being greeted by myriad serving staff. They seem very popular. I'm the anonymous one in this company.

My thoughts return to me. To my problem. V's foot is in my lap but her mind is elsewhere. As much as I want to use her perfectly poised toes to answer my needs, to push me over the edge, I can't. I need her to be aware, to know what's going on, to want to be involved. What was the most important thing in the world a second ago is forgotten. But my cock. My pulsating cock. Can I really stop the pleasure just like that?

The option is taken from me.

With a swift motion, V retracts her leg, slips into her shoes and is standing, walking gracefully towards the entrance, where Michael and Clarisse are still nodding hellos.

I sit frustrated. I have a thousand sensations raging around my cock, double that number of nerve endings just waiting for the trigger to end my pain, the single word needed to put me out of my misery. But it doesn't come. And neither do I.

I can't bear to look at our guests. They are the reason I'm in this state, but they're also the reason I'm in such discomfort. I feel my erection start to subside. My clothes suddenly seem a size too large. The freedom is crushing. I have tasted constriction and I enjoyed its promises.

I must regroup, get ready, be on my best behaviour, I think. Our friends mustn't have a clue what we've been up to.

I wonder how I'm going to stand to kiss Clarisse hello and shake Michael's hand without the whole restaurant seeing the state I'm in. But I don't get the chance. The *maître d'* is standing next to me. He is holding my coat and telling me that 'madame' has been taken ill and will meet me at the front of the restaurant.

I'm confused, but when I look over my three dining companions are nowhere to be seen. With my coat conveniently held in front of my stomach, I stand up and leave, thanking all and sundry on my way. 'What is going on?' I wonder. 'What is she up to?'

As I enter into the crisp night air, I'm aware of a black cab ticking over on standby beyond the photographers' patch. A door swings open and Michael hails me over.

'Good to see you, old man,' he says cheerily. 'Slight change of plan. Girls, eh?' He is as good-natured as he is good-looking. I enter the cab, take my place opposite the others on one of the pull-down seats facing backwards, and reach over to kiss Clarisse. She looks more radiant than usual, a low-cut floral number pinching precisely in all the areas she wants to highlight. From where I'm looking, that's all of them. She really is a stunning woman. My fantasy of earlier floods my mind for a second, but I clear the image. I've had enough false starts this evening. I don't think my cock could take another unfulfilled rude awakening.

V calls out to the driver and the cab pulls away. We make small talk. It's good to see them again. Then V changes the subject.

'I hope you don't mind, but I told Clarisse about your little dream,' she purrs. She's looking for a reaction in my face. I know this, but I can't stop giving her what she wants.

'What little dream?' I bluff, but nobody is convinced.

'Anyway,' V continues, 'poor Clarisse was so shocked that she refused to eat with you tonight. And Michael wasn't too keen either.'

I flash a glance at Clarisse's husband, and I'm met with the steely glare from his dark brown eyes. How annoyed is he? How likely is he to kick up over this? What are the odds of her taking offence and never talking to me again?

Very low, I think.

'So, this dream,' Clarisse says. 'Was I dressed like this?'

I don't know what to say. So I smile and say nothing. I think it's the right answer.

'Or maybe I was dressed more like this?' she continues, and slowly reaches her left hand over to her right shoulder and peels off the thin diamante strap, before doing the same on the opposite shoulder. A sharp jerk of her upper torso, and the front of her dress falls down as far as her breasts. She must be cold. Her nipples snag the soft material as it falls, her pert tits deliciously on show and yet hiding under the folded dress. The cab hits a bump in the road and the unveiling is completed. Both breasts are completely exposed, completely brown and sunwashed, completely inviting me to stare at them.

'Is this what I looked like?' she asks again. 'Is this jogging your memory?'

I can't take my eyes off her amazing tits. So animated in the rocky cab ride, so upwardly pointing, so incredibly sexy. I look at Michael, who just stares back and smiles. V winks. Clarisse puts her index finger in her mouth and sucks. Then she rubs it underneath each nipple before putting it back in her mouth.

I feel hot. It's unbearable in the taxi suddenly. I start to sweat. Clarisse notices.

'You look uncomfortable,' she says. 'Perhaps you should loosen some clothing.'

Before she has even finished saying that, she falls forward from her scooped cab seat and lands on her knees in front of me. Her hands work like a concert pianist's over my trousers, expertly unzipping the straining fly. With her next swift movement she slides a hand inside, and for the first time this evening I feel a hand wrap around my cock. It feels so good.

So direct. It feels incredible to be squeezed like that, like she wants to crush me, to bring me under her power, to make me obey her.

I am in her thrall. I have been since before she arrived.

'Naughty man, making us miss out on dinner,' she says. 'I'm so hungry.'

I'm sure I've heard that line in a film and it sounded cheesy. But right now, with her freeing my cock from the bondage of my shorts and trousers, licking her lips and staring down ravenously, it's the sexiest thing anyone has ever said to me.

'Oh, Clarisse . . .' It's all I can manage. For the second time this evening my ability to speak has been halted. I'm on mute. Her mouth has hit the button that stops all communication.

She's licking me, holding me with her left hand, jerking me violently up and down, and running her tongue along the line exposed by the grasping fingers. I feel her hot tongue lash over my straining skin, then disappear as she tastes her own fingers, then back down again on me. I close my eyes. I dare not look at the woman of my dreams, literally, with her head in my lap, her tongue swirling over my most sensitive parts, kissing my tip, plunging down several inches, then sucking, just sucking, pulling all thoughts of pleasure up my shaft as she withdraws, guiding all sensation in the direction of her mouth.

I've never felt so helpless. I've never felt so desperate to be pleasured and yet so intimidated by my environment. V, of course, delights in such wildness. But this is new to me. It's virgin territory for me to be sucked by the wife of one of my best friends, while he watches, and with a cab driver inches from my own head.

What is Michael thinking? What must he be thinking as he sees Clarisse lower her mouth so far down my shaft that I feel the wall at the back of her mouth? Oh, this is extraordinary? No one has been able to take me so far, no one has let me rub against the opening of their throat. She kisses me, and draws her lips up my hyperventilating shaft, but at the same time I'm being stimulated by the direct and unexpected pressure on my head as it slides across the back of her mouth.

What must Michael think?

I open my eyes for a second. I see what Michael thinks. I see him unzipping his own trousers and trying to stand up in the back of the cab. I see V kiss his outstretched cock as it passes irresistibly in front of her face. I see him taking his place behind his wife and run his hands from the arch of her shoulders down her back, massaging the perfect curves of her waist, her hips, her tightly round arse and down further, down the back of her thighs. I see him slide his hands underneath the hem of her dress and lift it up, folding it neatly on to the small of her back. I see she wears no underwear there either. She is the ideal mannequin. Anything extra would spoil the lines.

It's all I can do to view the scene before me. I can't process the information. I am a camera without film. I see Michael manoeuvre his cock with one hand and steady himself against Clarisse's hip with the other, but all I feel is the slowing of her tongue on my own cock. I see him place his second hand just below her waist but all I feel is Clarisse's hot breath burning my wet head. I see Michael brace himself then push forwards by several inches, but all I feel is Clarisse sink further down my cock, her mouth open in a silent scream. For a second I have lost her. Her thoughts are not with me. But just for a second.

'Oh, Mikey, oh, Mikey . . .' She's talking to him but she's staring at me. She's speaking to the man fucking her from behind, but she's holding my cock and lapping at her spit run down it, mingled with my own juices. She talks to him but through me, without taking her eyes off me. I'm her microphone.

I don't know how long this goes on. Sometimes Clarisse lurches forwards unexpectedly, sometimes she is in total control. Sometimes the cab's sudden motions throw the three of us into unpredicted angles, but sometimes it's the power of Michael from behind, driving her forwards and down on my cock. Sometimes it's him enticing her to push her arse back as far as she can to meet his thrusts, while he reaches round and squeezes her swinging breasts, pulling on her exposed nipples, holding them for balance and for love, but taking her mouth away from me for that moment. The agony of her withdrawal is compensated by the vision of her face racked in ecstasy, until she returns and the pleasure becomes mine.

My night gets more unbelievable by the second.

And it's about to get better.

V has watched so far. I know this has been her plan. I know she must have suggested this to our friends. But I don't know what she's going to do.

But she does.

The rattling unsteadiness of the cab only adds to my pleasure as Clarisse works on my cock, but it throws V off balance as she tries to stand up. Her head is bent over, but she rests on my shoulder. Her back is to me and she edges back closer, lifting a leg over my lap, now straddling me, forcing the small of her back into my face. I don't hear any words, but I know she must be in discomfort, bent almost double by the roof of the cab. My own pain is growing as she presses my head back against the dri-ver's partition glass. I can't think about him, though.

I can only think about the hand around my cock.

Now I can only think about V's pussy as she lowers her weight and sends my penis into raptures of new and unexpected delight. I was being sucked by Clarisse and now I'm being fucked by V.

What a night.

V's shoulders are level with my mouth and I start to kiss her there. Responding to her moans, I kiss harder, biting a little, kissing some more. I can nearly reach her neck. She has her hands on the roof of the cab to steady herself, but really she uses the position to force her weight down on my lap, down on my cock. She doesn't bounce up and down, she doesn't have room. She grinds her pelvis forwards, then squeezes back, swallowing me inside her, drawing me further in. She's a belly dancer, rhythmically rolling her lower body, using her bent arms to push down from the roof on to me, impaling me, using me to fill her.

I am blind. I see flashes of the others in the darkened side windows, but the movements are blurry, indistinct. The forms are shaky like reflections in a pool of water, in strict contradiction to the precision of their movements.

I run my hands around the front of V's waist, and let them drift lower, between her straining legs. I want to feel the softness of her inner thigh. I want to run my fingers down to that point where she and I join, where she and I become one. I want to feel with my fingers what I can't see, what I can only imagine from the sensations in my cock.

But I can't do it. I can't reach. There's something in the way. It's hair. It's Clarisse. Her hands are resting on V's thighs, keeping them apart, steadying her so she can lower her face to V's pussy, to run her tongue down its frenzied maw, to taste the shared lust that oils her movements, that drives her further on to me.

I feel Clarisse's tongue. She's on me, licking me, and then it disappears. She must be kissing V's beautiful pussy now, licking her clitoris, lapping across in patterns and swirls that drive both women crazy.

It's working. I know it's working. I feel V's legs tighten, I see the ripples in her arms become more defined as she forces herself against the roof of the car. She can't push down hard enough. She doesn't know what she wants. Her legs propel her one way, her arms the other. Her weight on my lap doubles, her back crushes my head sideways against the driver's partition. My neck is twisted and I struggle to breathe. I'm aware of it, but I feel nothing.

I only feel the building momentum at the core of my body, at that point where I become V and we become Clarisse. That point where V's pussy feeds her friend's ravenous tongue and engulfs me in its deepest, tightest, hottest pleasure.

There's noise now. I hear slaps of hand on flesh. I hear Clarisse respond to Michael's touch. I hear breathing working up, I hear growls and sighs and moans and howls. I hear hands punching against the lined cab roof, I hear my own head imprinted noisily against the plastic glass.

I hear screams.

I hear howls.

I hear the rush of blood from my head as it rages through my entire body. I hear the surge of energy explode in me and in V at the same time. I hear the siren of Clarisse's orgasm cut the night air. I hear Michael's plaintive 'Oh, fuck!' as he loses his balance and collapses on his wife's arched back. I hear V sniffle as her body reminds her to breathe, as her backup battery kicks in to drive her short gulps of air until she is back in control.

I feel her relax and I can ease my face away from the glass and move my arms round to support her body as she sits there, on me, drained of life. I am still hard inside her. I am still pulsing, squeezing new sensation out of my body, shivering to a close.

I hear silence.

I hear the sounds of the world start to creep into our car. I hear tyres and engines and the voices of pavement walkers. I am awake. I am back in the real world. I am in agony in my neck. But it doesn't matter. My memories will heal any physical wound. I still feel invincible, a foot taller at least.

A few minutes pass before we start to extricate ourselves from this game of sexual Twister. We are all weary. Clarisse's dress is torn and her knees look raw. V is shivering, cold with the evening's invasive temperature. Michael and I lean back and try to re-dress. Silence permeates the cab. Serenity has taken hold. I can't help touching myself, recalling the two women who have just caused such pleasure. I can't help bringing my fingers to my lips, to taste V's sugary traces and enjoy the feast of flavours that Clarisse had enjoyed.

I don't know where the cabbie is taking us, but I do know his meter turned off long ago. He won't be charging for this journey. I would pay the Earth for that experience but he won't take a penny.

V

V IS FOR VIOLATION

I like traditions. I like shared happiness, the more exclusive the better. I like Christmas and birthdays, but I prefer those little routines that friends or lovers have, those little rituals that mean nothing to anyone else, but everything to you. A couple of my friends like catching those open-top tourist buses whenever they go to a new town. I think it's naff, but it's something they've always done. Others like snuggling up to *Book at Bedtime* together, or walking the dog. Personal things, like pet names, that tie you together.

And then there's V. She likes to tell me everything. I'm her confidant and her confessor. She doesn't have guilt, but she still prefers her activities to be secret from certain people. But she has to tell someone. She has to share her excitement with someone else. And, by and large, that someone is me.

Sometimes she'll tell me of her hopes. Sometimes she'll tell me of a new adventure she's had. Sometimes she'll want to ask my advice. Or sometimes, like now, she'll call when she's on her way out to meet a stranger she encountered on the Internet.

'What do you know about him?' I ask.

'I know he likes blondes.'

'Are you blonde at the moment?'

'No! I'm looking on it as a challenge. I want him to get over himself. By the time I'm finished, he won't know what colour is.'

She laughs but I believe her.

'I'll call you later,' she says. 'I think I'll need to talk.'

That was several hours ago. In the middle I had a work emergency. But V is as good as her word. She calls, and when I don't pick up, she leaves a message. It's not the longest message I've ever received – she recorded that last year. But it's probably too long for the memory on my phone. Which is a shame. I hate to miss the endings. She always tones it down the day after. And I like to hear from her when she's fresh from her encounters. When the smell of her conquest is alive on her skin, when her clothes have another's odour dominating her own fragrance. I like to hear from her with her heart still racing, when her imagination is fired, her body sated.

A vodka over ice in my hand, my feet up on the sofa. I press play and sit back. *Book at Bedtime* has nothing on Radio V . . .

Hello, are you going to pick up? It's me, pick up please. Oh, God, where are you? Not to worry, if you hear this, just pick up when you can, otherwise I'll just rabbit into your machine.

Did I tell you he liked blondes?

When I arrived, he was with two of them, standing outside a bar. A boy and a girl. They looked like twins. He said they were both dancers. I asked if I was interrupting anything and do you know what he said? 'We're just deciding which one of them stays. Have you got a coin?'

I thought he was joking. But he tossed a fifty-pence piece into the air and, as it fell, said, 'Heads, she stays, tails, it's him.'

It was all so quick. I hadn't really had a chance to examine either of them. In fact from what I could see, I'd rather they both stayed and he cleared off. But as I said, it was so quick. The coin hit the ground on its edge and lurched off into the road. Two cars went by before we could find it. When we did, it was heads. Woo-hoo.

The blond guy kissed us all before he left. When he got to me I whispered I'd like to see him soon, hopefully for longer next time. He gave me such a quizzical smile and said I'd have to ask his sister. See, I was right! Twins. But he gave me a kiss on the lips that I won't forget in a hurry. It was like he wanted to kiss my soul. Have you ever been kissed like that? With two hands gently cradling your face, someone staring into your eyes as they approach, dropping their lids closed at the last moment, and you know they're thinking of you in their darkness. Have you ever felt your life flash in front of your eyes as you give in to someone else's touch?

But he was leaving! If he kisses like that when he's going, what's he like when he's coming!

I admit, I was more than a little horny now. I couldn't take my eyes off his arse as he walked away, but then I realized, 'I've got two birds in the hand here. Let's see if they're worth more than the one in the bush.'

'Do you have a plan?' I asked. Silly question.

What a silly question. This guy has his whole life mapped out to the second. It's a bit scary, don't you think? I couldn't live like that. Where's the adventure in knowing what you're doing? I love the feeling that life is like being the ice cube shaken around a Martini glass. Who knows where I'll end up?

This guy gets his kicks from order. He gets off on knowing that two people are coming to see him, and they're going to be his toys for the next couple of hours. He's got his rituals, down to the last minute. Who knew sex could be so scientific?

I don't know if it was his house or he was a guest

like the rest of us, but we ended up in a room at a party. It was one of those black and white affairs, everyone in penguin suits and cocktail dresses. But there was something odd there. He said hello to a couple of people, and led the way across the large lounge into a side room. I felt every pair of eyes in the room staring at this odd caravan – the guy, the blonde, and yours truly.

The room was something else. I don't know if it could be called a room, really. It was a laboratory. A laboratory for sexual experimentation. He was the scientist and he'd decided I would be his assistant. The blonde was our guinea pig for the night.

Part of me wished I was the guinea pig, but that wasn't my choice. There was a lot of leather in this laboratory. There was so much to take in at first that I didn't notice the giant X-shaped construction next to the fireplace. I didn't notice the blonde begin to disrobe, without a word being passed between us. I didn't see her step back on to the X, and let him clasp her wrists and ankles with the built-in feather-lined leather restraints. I was so engrossed in the array of dildos and whips and chains and masks and plug-in toys that I had no idea this was going on behind me. They were so silent. It was like a proper lab, I'm sure. Imagine my surprise when I turned round and saw this kinky crucifixion ready to kick off behind me!

I'm not a religious person, not in the traditional sense, you know that. I say 'God' and 'Jesus' sometimes, but only when I'm horny, only when I'm being pleasured beyond my wildest dreams. Is there a better word when you're out of control of your own body, and someone else is in charge of your feelings? Is that wrong? Those words just have sexual connotations for me now. So when I saw this cross, with this naked woman pinned to it, I didn't think anything except, 'What a practical contraption!'

Oh, and that she wasn't a natural blonde too.

The man gave me a white coat, made of rubber, and suggested I put it on if I wanted to take part in the experiment. He also 'suggested' it would fit better if it didn't have to stretch over clothes. I'm not a shy person and, let's face it, there was a naked woman strapped to a leather X in front of me, but something about this sterile environment, with all its spotlights and clean, metal implements, made me self-conscious. I've never felt that before. Isn't that weird? I've never worried about what people might think, especially if I'm taking my clothes off.

I think I was being coy!

I turned my back on the pair of them as I stepped out of my skirt and pulled my blouse over my head. Suddenly the nerves left me and I began to enjoy myself. I couldn't see behind me, so I could imagine what they were thinking. I was putting on a show for them, I realized. I needed to perform.

I was standing there in my shoes, stockings and underwear and I knew exactly how hot I looked from behind. I knew that the cream lace strapping of my bra crisscrossed so precisely against my tanned back, and that the peaches of my arse teased half out of the coquettish briefs.

The bra came off first. I hooked each shoulder strap down slowly, sliding a thumb under each one, then holding my hands out in front of me, shimmying my body to shake the supports down. Then I reached round and unclasped. For a second nothing moved. Suction and accurate measurements held the bra to my breasts. Slowly I started to lean forwards, watching as the hoops of my straps fell down, but still the cups stayed in place. I was nearly at right angles to my legs, I was starting to feel the burn in my cheeks, my breasts were building gradual momentum, starting to swing side to side, and finally I felt the loosening of the cups' grip on my titties as, left one first, then right, they came off, almost in slow motion, like a man desperately clinging for his life to a cliff edge.

The subtle release caused my breasts to collide and they surprised me with their movements, trembling into each other, then shimmering apart. They felt heavy, sensitive to the air around them after such close contact all day, and alive. Every inch of my skin felt like it wanted to be touched, like it needed to be comforted, to be held by another.

I was a stripper now. I was a table dancer, I expected dollar bills in my suspender belt by the time I turned round. But first I had to slide out of my knickers, out of my shoes, out of my stockings, out of my belt. Only now did I take the opportunity to glance over my shoulder at my audience.

The man had his back to me!

What's his fucking problem? I thought. But that's all part of his game, isn't it? He 'suggested' I put the coat on. He hadn't built time in for my burlesque. If he'd wanted a floor show, he would have suggested it.

I was a little girl again. I was being told off. I expected him to turn, look me in the eye and say, 'I'm not angry – I'm disappointed.'

But then I saw the girl, studying me with a mix of hunger and impatience. I saw her run her tongue along the underneath of her top lip, and I was restored. I zipped up the white coat as best I could, feeling myself pour into the rubber, feeling my breasts resist the ungiving material across my chest, and smiling as the zip began to edge back down, tooth by tooth, as the rise and fall of my breathing gave my titties a life of their own. They would not be constrained by this rubber coat. But maybe that was the plan.

'I've started without you,' the man said coolly. 'You'll have to pay more attention in future.'

Oh, he was a cool one.

'I want to test her response to different materials,' he said. 'Use those items on her. I want you to get a reaction. Don't listen to her mouth, listen to her body. Tell me what you see. Remember, use your eyes, not your ears. Can you do that?'

I nodded. I was fascinated. There was a surgical trolley next to him – there were so many things on it I'd never seen before and some that were very familiar.

My eye fell on the ice bucket, complete with tongs. 'We'll start with this,' I said, trying to take control.

'Be very precise with your actions,' he told me, instantly reasserting himself. 'If you do it wrong the whole experiment is wasted.'

I didn't really hear him, I was so fascinated by what I had to do. I tweezed a cube of ice with the tongs and held it in front of the blonde. She was looking directly into my eyes, trying to communicate with me without words. But what was she saying? I had no idea. Not yet.

I stepped forwards so I was inches from her beautiful naked body, and rested the ice against the crook of her neck. She squealed, but that was not what I was looking for. At the same time, instinctively, her neck flicked over to smother the freezing sensation, but then a second later it pulled upright, allowing me total access to her beautiful collarbone, her tiny ear, her straining, tense neck. I ran the cube up and down, watching her face. She tried to look into my eyes but couldn't. She closed her eyes and I studied her face as she bit her bottom lip, and opened her mouth to expel the tiniest of expressions. 'Ooh,' 'Mmm,' 'Oh!'

I looked down. Her nipples were surprisingly large for her smallish breasts, and they stood to attention now. What would happen if I moved the ice along her arm? Nothing. What would happen if I dragged it, beginning to melt now, back along the shoulder to the small of the neck, and up to the erogenous nerve centre behind her ear? Oh, a wonderful result. Those tiny, downy hairs around her nipples were electrified and her skin strained harder than I thought possible. If I touched her breasts, I felt, I could be injured. They looked sharp. They looked like they could cut skin. They looked like they could penetrate without trying.

I thought I would come back to the ice, because this cube was melting. But I still had the tongs.

'Oh, that is very good,' the man said. 'I hadn't thought of that one.'

I didn't care what he had thought of. I was in

charge now. The ice had gone, but the metal tongs were still icy cold. I ran the back of the claw, the smooth part, down the line of the blonde's neck. She winced at the touch, but I saw her lip bitten again. I ran it down her front, to her left breast, and underneath. I took the weight of her bosom on the tong, and lifted as far as it would reach. Then I pulled away and watched her titty fall and bounce back up again. There is no other thing on Earth that has the movement patterns of a firm breast. Size doesn't play a part. You can't replicate that deep shuddering. The sight of breasts moving, in clothes or unbound, is unique. It fascinates me; I can watch my own knock gently together like a sensual Newton's cradle, and be aroused every time. I don't require any touch, just the vision of my own body moving, beckoning, stirring my thoughts.

Vision is what I'd been ordered to use. I ran the back of the tong up her perky bosom, to the vicious-looking nipple that stared angrily, defiantly at me. I had caused its erectness, and I must pay, it seemed to say. I can't tell you how much I wanted to touch that nipple with my fingers, how much I wanted to plant my hand on her breast and feel the firmness of her nipple slide between two outstretched fingers. I so wanted to bend and kiss, and suck, and perhaps even bite. My pussy was telling me to. I don't know what was greater, the desire to kiss her or touch myself. But I had my instructions.

I picked up a feather next, and marvelled at how much resistance could be generated by something so light. I saw the man nod with approval at every shudder, every flinch. And I saw the excitement building in his trousers. I went to touch him but he made it clear that was out of bounds. I had work to do.

A whip, a cat-o'-nine-tails, was handed to me. The ends had tiny knots, little pockets of pain waiting to be shared with the unsuspecting victim. But this blonde was not unsuspecting. And she was no victim. I've never seen a woman respond to the lash of nine individual flails with such excitement. Six times I swung at her. Once over her chest, which sent a contortion of pain through her body. But five more times over her thighs, stinging leather lashes raining down around her most sensitive area, enervating her, invigorating her, causing her to push her groin as far out from the X as the binding on her arms and legs would allow. She liked this. She liked the nine tiny spikes lacerating her skin (superficially, I hope), the not knowing where they would fall, the pinpricks of diverting pain and yet exquisite ecstasy as her pussy received messages from all round. I admit, I was confounded by her reaction. She took the punishment and turned it into an orgasm of relief. How was this possible? I couldn't wait to try it myself.

I picked up a candle next. Close by it was a metal item that I couldn't identify, and a studded vibrator. I shivered to think of that mediaeval torture implement entering me and I couldn't imagine forcing it on anyone else. But I knew I could have some fun with the hot wax. I've enjoyed it myself on many occasions.

The thing about candles is they're not precise instruments. You hold them here, they drop wax there. You aim for the top of her pussy, it runs down your hand and you end up coating her belly. But that's what I like. And I think that's what the blonde liked.

The X that she was pinned to was not as simple as I suspected. It was actually on a pivot. The whole machine could spin if you pushed hard enough. I didn't know this until the man reached out to the wooden column supporting the blonde's left arm, and leaned firmly on it. Immediately she started to move anticlockwise; within seconds her right arm was where her head had been. A few seconds more and she was upside down. Where her delectable, enticing mouth had been, I was now staring at her beautiful raven-haired pussy.

A thought occurred to me. She was my target, I was the knife thrower. I took two steps back and nodded to the man to spin the wheel of fortune one more time. This time he did it harder, and I watched her body swing upside down, then back again, her breasts falling this way and that, but still alive with that unique movement.

As she started her second rotation, I flicked the candle towards her. 'Ouch!' she cried. Again I did it, and more molten wax speckled her exposed frame. Once more she whelped. Once more I sprayed her tiny form with my burning liquid.

The flame went out at that point, but the candle was still hot. I had ideas raging through my body now, and I reached my spare hand into the ice bucket and took a cube into my mouth. It was so cold. How long can you hold ice in your mouth without dropping it?

Who was I punishing? Her or me?

I leaned on one of the X crossbeams, and spun the blonde upright. Her nipples were what I wanted. I bent forwards and rested my icy lips on her breast, feeling them spring to firmness. The blonde emitted a shrill yelp, but still I went on, reaching over and trying to kiss the other nipple. Then I pulled back and held the candle close to the frozen area I had just left. Slowly, the last piece of liquid wax moved to the rim of the candle, and just fell. It landed squarely on her erect nipple and she screamed. She really, really screamed.

That noise sent a charge through my body. It was like my ears were between my legs. Her voice spoke directly to my pussy and I felt my pussy respond, with tiny palpitations, little quivers. I knew I was wet, I knew I was ready for more direct personal requirements. But would I get the chance?

I threw the candle aside, much to the man's irritation, and gave the wheel another spin. Her pussy was now where her head had been. Her splayed legs gave me an almost medical view. But no doctor sees a patient in this condition. I could see the physical reaction to her suffering and her squeals of excitement beginning to seep from between her lips. Her tiny hairs glistened with the dew of lust and I couldn't take my eyes off them. I wanted to run my tongue along that line of silky moisture, and take it into my mouth, and taste her love for me at that moment.

I bent forwards to kiss her, but it wasn't my tongue that she felt, it was the ice, barely formed now, but solid enough to send her body into violent spasms of delirious agony. I expected steam to rise from her lips as her volcanic desire met my frozen kiss.

But the only thing that rose was my temperature. That stupid rubber coat was annoying me, clinging to me when I wanted to be free. I pulled my shoulders back and the zip immediately fell by a couple of inches, exposing the double roundness of my breasts. I yanked it further down, until the coat was totally open, and I stepped towards the blonde.

I didn't say anything. But she could see as much of me as I could see of her. If I angled myself well, she could reach me too.

I swirled my tongue around my mouth and removed the residues of ice. It was still cold in there, but I would soon be warm, I knew that. I leaned fully against the blonde, and felt the piercing of her belly-button rub awkwardly just above my pubis as I tried to lower myself against her. I had her pussy inches from my mouth, I wanted mine just as close to her. She would have to work her neck muscles to get anywhere near me, but if she didn't, I would stop. I really prayed that message would be enough.

I dipped my tongue into the crowning aperture of her pussy. She was so wet, her lips were already parting. Tectonic plates of desire, shifting with nature, moving majestically to prepare for new experiences. I felt her shudder as the coolness of my touch spread around her body, but she soon acclimatized. I heard her murmur, but felt her relax. I pushed down deeper, and felt the heat of her pussy juices rising up my tongue like water through paper. I was being warmed up, fired up by her burning loins. I don't know if it was the feather or the whip or the ice or the wax, but this woman was ready for anything.

And so was I. It was her chin I felt first. I could sense her body tighten as she lifted her head up, desperate to reach me with her tongue. But we were both trapped in our own way, she by leather binding, me by proximity to her pussy. So she improvised, rubbing her small, round chin between my crouched legs. Where I used precision, she wielded a flat tool, but it was all I needed at that moment.

I groaned aloud, and didn't care what the man thought. The blonde was the guinea pig, not me. I could make all the fucking noise I wanted to, and she had better be listening.

'Oh, that is amazing,' I yelled. This wasn't an accident. She was really working my clit with her chin. I could feel the soft skin stretched over bone, the velvet glove over the iron fist, and I responded. I ground myself down, pushing against her face, praying that her neck muscles would last. I just needed another minute, I just needed to concentrate all my energies on that furnace between my legs.

But I couldn't ignore her. I reached round the back of the X and steadied myself, using the sturdy support to clamp my mouth to the pussy bath displayed to me. I knew I had to be precise, I knew I had to use my tongue to sweep up her juice, to swallow it, to massage her with my face while she did the same to me, but I just wanted to dive in. I wanted to bury my nose in her pussy, I wanted to smear my face with her ointment, feel her stickiness cling to my cheeks and my lips and my chin when I pulled back. I wanted to flick her clit with my eyelids as I blinked. I wanted to breathe into her vagina, to tantalize her, and prepare her for my warm touch.

I wanted to do so much, I really did, but she was working so hard on me that I knew my time was limited. I started to kiss her hole in earnest, imagining it was her brother's mouth, really exploring with my tongue, and pushing down on her eager clit with the underneath of my throat, with my chin, with my jaw. I felt her starting to shake and I knew I was close too. I pressed harder, and felt her do the same. I released my grip and sensed her relax too. I buried my face again in her stifling delights and then I felt the charge shoot through her body as she tightened and loosened, gripped and let go, pushed and pulled at the same time. She was thrashing around with her head, beating my pussy with everything she could reach with, and it worked. I was sent over the top, sent to heaven and back to Earth on a yo-yo, again and again.

I felt her pulsing vagina squirm against my touch and wanted to kiss it more and more. But she was tender now. My next kiss brought a cry of 'stop' from her, and I knew that enough was enough. I stepped back and turned the wheel. She returned to an upright position but looked drained. The colour had left her face. It was all between her legs.

I kissed her on the lips just as her brother had kissed me, and she rubbed noses with me. Immediately I could smell my own sex on her, and it thrilled me, having it on me, daubed with my own aroma, carried around on my nose for the rest of the night.

I dressed, once more overcome with shyness, and turned to find the blonde wearing a different, but equally sexy outfit.

'I'll show you out,' the man said. 'Follow me.'

I wasn't paying any attention to him as he swung open the door, I was watching the blonde scampering behind him. But when I did look, the lounge had been transformed. The dinner-suit brigade I had seen earlier were nowhere to be seen. Everywhere I looked were naked couples, and triples and more, playing with each other. A man and woman there, two men and a woman there, three women in a circle next to them, five men and a single girl somewhere else.

And over there was the blond brother.

'This way, V,' the man said. 'I'll escort you to your car.'

'Hang on a minute,' I replied. 'There's someone over there I want to say hello to.'

So guess what I did? Oh, don't bother trying, I'm sure you're sick of my voice now. I'll tell you when I see you. Call me, darling. Kiss kiss.

VI

V IS FOR VOYEUR

V wants me to do her a favour. She wants me to check her emails. She's given me the passwords, everything I need to know to get into her virtual desktop, to enter her virtual life. It's a new dimension in our relationship. We've shared so much, but I've never had a glimpse into this side of her. She tells me about her e-lovers, she describes what they get up to, how they write, how they fantasize about each other. But she's never written to me, I've never written to her, and she's never shown me any of her correspondence.

Until now.

She needs a number and an address. It's an emergency, obviously, otherwise she wouldn't have asked me. I don't know what the information is for, just where to find it.

Her email world is new territory for me. There is a section for her charity work, another for family. An area for business and banking, another for various media projects.

And there is my name. Twice. There's a folder with

my name on, just as a label. And another that says it is
for me. It says it's for my eyes only. I wonder what it
is. A shiver runs up my spine. It's like a will. In the
event of something happening to V, retrieve this
folder. Protect her memory. Her legacy.

My mind wanders. Did she plan this? Did she call
me on purpose, wanting me to see these folders?
Is tonight the night she intended to hand it over?

I can't think about that now, I have to find the
number. Here it is. I find my mobile and punch the
information into a text. I hope it reaches her in time.

A minute later I receive a text reply. She has the
info. I've saved her life. She'll call me later to explain.

She'll call me later.

She'll call me later.

What if she doesn't call me later? What if she has
no intention of calling anyone ever again? What if I've
already spoken my last words to her? What if she
wanted me to read her emails?

So many thoughts carousel around my mind.
I know there is nothing wrong, but it has become an
irritating obsession. I go back to the computer. I re-key
her passwords and re-enter the virtual world of V.

The folder marked with my name catches my eye
first. I open it and am amazed to find more than a
thousand files. The numbers are staggering. What
could be in them?

I scroll down. Some are from ten or so years ago. V had internet access before anyone else I know. But I didn't. I couldn't have written to her then.

I click randomly on a file dated '11/8/93'. It's labelled 'chapel' and I'm unsure what it will reveal.

The message appears on the screen and suddenly everything makes sense. These are not messages from me to her. They are notes, memories about me. They are electronic diary entries.

And I am reading them.

I should close the account now, but the urge to know more about my beloved V is overwhelming. And, after all, it is about me, about our childhood so long ago. I'll just read this one and shut down the computer. Just this one.

I remembered that time we played in the chapel today. I think I saw a similar one on some MTV video and it triggered the memory. I'd forgotten how striking he was then. So powerful, so rangy and tall. He seemed to turn from a podgy kid into this heartbreaker overnight. Why didn't I notice it earlier? All those times we played together. All those times I told him about the boys I fancied, and he just nodded and gave me his opinion. And all the time he was better-looking than the rest of them, and nicer. All those times we cuddled like brother and sister under the moonlight in the garden. Why didn't we lean over and remember we were teenagers desperate to experiment? Why didn't we both see that the person we should have been losing our cherries to was right next to us?

I can still see the chapel now. I don't recall when Grandfather built it, or why, but I know I was the only one who used it. And not for praying in.

I had so many good times there. That was where I ran to when I wanted to hide, when I wanted to escape from the world. That was where I read my favourite books and stored my most treasured toys. That was where I talked about the birds and the bees with my girlfriends, and him of course. And that was where I lost my virginity to Tom B. (Sorry, Grandfather!)

I was so prepared. I was wearing my best outfit, my Sunday best in fact, which was appropriate for our small chapel. I don't think Tom knew what he was letting himself in for, although he claimed he did. Men don't change. A bluffer is a bluffer is a bluffer.

I thought he was trying to twist my nipples right off. He seemed fascinated by them. No one else had ever touched them before. I knew that I could come just by teasing them if I did it long enough. I presumed he knew that too. But he didn't know anything. He spent so long playing with my breasts that he came in his pants. I've never seen anyone so embarrassed. He looked like he'd peed himself. There was so much of it. I think he had a lifetime's worth stored up there.

The look on his face will stay with me forever. He went from faux Casanova to a teenager who wanted to cry. I wanted to laugh so much but I was still horny, so I hugged him and told him it was all right. (Ha! That was the last time I ever said those words!)

And then the door opened and I was suddenly grateful that we hadn't gone any further. I pulled my blouse down and looked presentable enough for adult eyes. But it wasn't an adult. It was him. My best friend.

I wonder why he turned up that day? He's always been there for me. I sometimes think he can sense when something's wrong. I think he can actually read my mind. If he was the kind of guy who could wire a plug I might actually think he bugged my house. He knows that much.

But I was so grateful to see him that day. I don't think I could have done it without him.

Stupid little me, not seeing the bigger picture. I was so busy wanting to fuck, it didn't occur to me that the idiot Tom wasn't the only option at that moment. Stupid, stupid little me.

Can you believe what happened next? I get giddy remembering the look on Tom's face when I said he was going to fuck me – and he was going to listen to instructions from my best friend or I would tell the whole village that he'd shot in his pants.

That poor kid. He did as he was told and he took his clothes off. I think he just stopped himself folding them and putting them neatly on one of the tiny pews. His cock was pretty good – I'd never seen a hard one before, not naked, and his seemed to be everything I'd hoped for, even though it wasn't fully up.

Then the instructions started. I don't know how he did it. I don't know how he kept a straight face. I wish he'd just told Tom to piss off and taken over himself. But he didn't. He was my friend. My very best friend. So he helped me out and did the next best thing, calling out what Tom should do.

'Stroke the breasts, slowly, gently, and cup your hand underneath, to take the weight in your palm, and pull them up to your mouth, so you can kiss the nipples, softly at first, then harder, harder like you want to kiss them back to life, then start to suck, gently again, watching her face all the time, looking for her reaction, listening to her breathing, alert to the signs that she likes your tongue on her hard, pink nipples, she's giving her body over to you, she trusts you to turn her on, to pleasure her, to make her safe, to make her come.'

The words stay with me today, the feeling even more so. The voice drifted from the other side of the room, but the touching was in front of me, on my own body. He was seducing me by remote control. And he was very good.

By the time Tom lay me down on the blanket I had prepared, I was ready. I was trepidatious, but excited, nervous but wet between my legs. I knew my body's signals even then. I knew I was ready for anything. After the hairbrush and the shoe and the vegetables and my brother's Action Men, I was no stranger to penetration. But on those times I was always in control. With Tom I had to give up power to him. He was the one kneeling between my legs. He was the one instructed to run his tongue down my body from my bellybutton, down through my bush, to my clit and down, deep into my pussy. Finally, we found something he could do well. Instinctively he buried his face in. He couldn't get enough. And neither could I. I promised myself then and there that I would have my pussy licked every day for the rest of my life. And a dozen years later I seem to have managed it. (But that's another story – actually a lot of stories!)

The voice from across the room stopped us. He was firm. He wanted Tom to pull back and sit up. He wanted Tom to place his hands on the ground beneath my armpits, as though he were about to do press-ups. He wanted Tom to kiss each nipple, and then look down, to where his ramrod cock was angling forwards, perfectly horizontal, and no more than six inches from my pussy. He wanted Tom to lower himself slowly, so the head of his cock nudged gently against my clit, then followed the same line down that his tongue had earlier done. He wanted Tom to stop and savour the new experience, the heat that burned from my pussy, the scalding hotness of my juices. He wanted Tom to dip his tip in, to gauge the sensation, and to let me know that he was there, that he was ready, and that I must be ready too.

And then he told Tom to lower himself further, while pulling his body forwards with his arms, and to embrace the velvety furnace of my pussy, and to enjoy it and to luxuriate in this rich, sugary bath of pure pleasure.

And he said, 'Look at V, Tom. Look at her eyes, see how she responds to being penetrated by you. See how the light in her eyes dazzles, how the pink spreads over her cheeks and how her mouth is shaped to say words that never come. Look at everything, Tom, and sense whether it's time to lower yourself on to her. Is it time to feel your pubic bone lock into hers, to feel your stomach cover her stomach, and your chest flat on top of hers? Sense whether she wants to kiss you, whether she wants to lock mouths with you as you lock cunt and cock. Sense if she's ready, Tom. Sense if she wants you to fuck.'

THE SECRET LIFE OF V

I think Tom's hearing had gone by this point. He was like an eel writhing up the beach as he threw his body up and down against mine, trying to get further inside my pussy. I didn't know what to expect from him, but I knew what I needed, and I sensed how to get it. The voice didn't need to tell me.

I sank my nails into Tom's shiny butt and pushed my arse up off the floor to meet his thrusts head on. With my feet planted firmly next to his knees, I used his weight to push his grinding where I needed it. I wanted his cock at the top of my pussy and his bone on my clit. I wanted friction, and I got it.

Tom came first, but I didn't care. I had him where I wanted him and I didn't let go till I'd locked my legs around him, squeezing the breath out of his body the way my pussy squeezed every last drop out of his cock.

I never fucked Tom again, but I got into the habit that day of discussing the sensation with my best friend. I wonder what would have happened if I'd fucked him instead? But this way I get the best of both worlds.

Wow. There's something eerie about hearing your own memories in someone else's words.

I remember that day vividly now. V had no idea how much it hurt me to watch that idiot soil her like that. But my pleasure was in making sure he did it right. I'm honoured she remembers it so fondly. But she's right. Would we still be friends now if I had been her first fuck? Maybe I'd be the one-off and Tom would be the one with access to her emails?

That blast of the present distracts me and I'm aware of how wrong it is to be snooping like this. But really, is there any harm? These are stories about me, after all. And I love V's little asides (in brackets!) in her writing. It's almost as though those are the bits of the real her. But the rest is there to be read. By me.

I decide to save the other messages for another time. The other folder intrigues me. The one marked for my eyes only.

There are many hundred of messages here, and it quickly becomes obvious they're not 'dear diary' pieces. Well, not like that. Each one is labelled with a name. Frank, Owen, Scott, Samuel, Keeley, Joel, Keeley and Joel . . . the list is endless. I guess they're chronological. I pick one at random. It's a name that seems familiar to me.

Maddox.

Odd name – it rings a bell, but is it a person or a place? Only one way to find out . . .

Dear Maddox

Thank you for your email. I wonder how you found me? I wonder if you know who I am? I wonder if you're ready for me? Do you think so, Maddox? Do you think your mind is mature enough for the thoughts I'm going to put in it? Do you think you can cope with the truth, Maddox? Do you think you can cope with the truth about love and romance and pain and death and love and romance and pain and sex? Do you think your mind is ready?

Do you think your body is ready for the things I'm going to do to it? Do you think you can lift a woman with just your erection, Maddox? Do you think you can lift me with your tongue when I climb on your shoulders and force my pussy against your face? Do you think you can walk with me there like that? Do you think you can breathe with my hands forcing your face into my bush, clamping your mouth and nose inside my pussy? Do you think you're strong enough, Maddox, to hold me upside down, with your tongue up my cunt, my knees dropped over your shoulders and my mouth mounting your cock? Have you ever 69-ed a woman standing up, Maddox? Have you ever felt the darkness of thighs pressing against your eyes, have you experienced the disorientation of trying to walk blind, of trying to concentrate on finding your way around with a woman's mouth sucking your beautiful cock? Have you, Maddox? Would you know what to do? Would you try to fuck my face or would you think that would throw your head backwards and push your balance out? Would you take the risk, Maddox, would you try to hump my mouth with your dirty, beautiful cock, would you try to thrust into me because I can't pull away? Would you take advantage of the fact I can't run? I can't move anywhere because you're holding me up. You've got me where you want me, you've got my pussy at your tongue's beck and call and you know I'll do anything to keep you kissing me there. Is that what you think, Maddox? Are you ready, Maddox?

I'm horny thinking about you, Maddox. Maybe I'll want to meet you. Maybe I'm going to touch myself now to see how I feel. Maybe if I enjoy it I'll give you an address and we can meet. Do you feel lucky, Maddox? Do you feel confident that if I touch myself between my legs I'm going to get off?

Maddox, I think this is your lucky day. I'm putting my fingers inside myself now, and I'm pulling them out slowly. I have three very wet, very hot, very sticky fingers here, Maddox. I'm going to lick them now. I'm going to suck them, one by one, and clean them. I think I'd like you to do this to me, Maddox. I think I'd like to feel you suck my fingers, darting your clever tongue around my knuckles, supping every drop. I think my fingers are stuck together, Maddox. I'm going to have to put two at once in my mouth. Could you handle two at once, I wonder?

I'm going to write an address now, Maddox. If you can be there within sixty minutes, you will make me very happy. If you can't be there, then I don't want you to contact me *again. I'm looking forward to this, Maddox. Meet me at . . .*

Curiouser and curiouser. But that's the name I remember. She had fun with him. He had a rubber fetish, which amused her. She could kick him down and he'd bounce back up.

I know she meets people on the Internet, but I had no idea this was how she presented herself. Funny. But so arousing. She reminds me of me when I read her words. We talk so much I don't know who sounds like who. But I do know she turns me on, even when she's not talking to me. I wonder what she did to Maddox that she didn't tell me? I'm going to have to read his story.

AFTERWORD

I've had an idea. I'm going to email her. I'm going to invent a name and send a wish to 'Mistress V'. Where's the address? Oh yes, V_is_for@hotmail.com.

Dear Mistress V

I dream about you. I dream about you every day. I've dreamed about you since I was six. When I was young I dreamed you were my sister. When I was older, I dreamed you were my girlfriend. Then you were my lover, my partner, my soul mate. I dreamed of kissing you from dawn till sunset, of buying you flowers every day we were apart, of playing your favourite songs every moment we are together.

I dream of being the special one in your life. I dream of another world, where I am the lover who made you a woman. Of another world where you can find satisfaction with one person, with me.

I dream I'm the person you talk about when you tell me your adventures in love. I dream I'm the one whose body you smother with kisses, whose prick you torment with ecstasy, whose face you hold with warm hands to kiss until I pass out with pleasure. I dream that the chance occasions where my presence has spilled over into your sexual life could last for ever. I dream that the times you let me touch your body, let me run my hands over your exquisite skin, let me dive inside your most private pool, are repeatable, again and again. I dream you want me as much as I want you.

I dream that when you're not with me, you want to be. And when you are with me, you're the happiest woman alive. And I am the happiest man.

You are my Venus. You always will be. You always have been.

Regards...

The 'send' button is there, beneath my cursor. But do I press? Do I tell her how I feel? Do I send? Do I risk everything?

What would you do?

What would you tell V? What dreams do you have that she could make true? What fantasies do you store in your mind to get you through the monotony of your day that you wish could be real?

What would you ask her?

What would you do?

Email V_is_for@hotmail.com if you dare . . .

Other books in the series:
Agent Provocateur: The Secret Life of I
ISBN 9781862057463

Further reading:
Agent Provocateur: Secrets
ISBN 1 86205 720 6

Agent Provocateur: Confessions
ISBN 1 86205 726 5

Agent Provocateur Exhibitionist
ISBN 1 86205 714 1

www.agentprovocateur.com